CHANGE OF KEY

CHANGE OF KEY

Africa to the Arts

MOIRA BENNETT

BITTERN PRESS

First published 2017
The Bittern Press
70 Firs Farm Cottages,
Off the Warren, Friston, Saxmundham
Suffolk IP17 1NS

Phototypeset by Agnesi Text, Hadleigh, Suffolk
Printed and bound in Great Britain by EAM Printers, Ipswich, Suffolk

A catalogue record for this book is available from the British Library.

ISBN 978 0 9571672 1 6

CONTENTS

FOREWORD

Kenneth Baird

There can be few people who have launched themselves into a profession at the age of fifty-four; and still fewer who – having begun work when many are thinking of early retirement – rise to the top of their chosen field.

After effectively inventing sponsorship of the arts in what was still a very rural part of England and raising a substantial endowment to secure the Aldeburgh Foundation's future, Moira Bennett proved so successful that she was asked to take on fundraising for the Barbican Centre and subsequently the London Symphony Orchestra. She was still working full-time for the LSO – which few would challenge was then unquestionably Britain's most distinguished symphony orchestra – into her seventies; when she eventually did decide to take on a slightly less pressured role, she was asked to become involved in a range of other important arts projects, pursuing these into her eighties. She has been described as the doyenne of fundraisers in the arts.

Now in her nineties, she tells the story of a notable life, which began in Africa. There are clues to her remarkable success: when self-doubt overcomes you, you tell yourself not to be so easily defeated; fundraising is just common sense; and, most of all, success depends on an understanding personal relationship with other people no matter how eminent. Her own international background has helped her relate to a wide range of people; as has the tragedy she has faced in her own life – tragedy that would have defeated many people lacking equivalent spirit.

Moira has an infectious sense of humour and this comes to the fore in this story told with vivacity. She has the ability to observe incidents dispassionately and gently to entertain the reader in their description. She also gives an insight into the realities of managing the performing arts – an insight the public is never usually given. I have not the slightest doubt that the story of Moira's remarkable life will both enlighten and entertain.

SOUTH AFRICA

T O START WRITING this memoir and to look back to where it all began is immediately to be struck by how far distant the beginning is. The world of ninety years ago, and particularly the world into which I was born, is almost unrecognisable and the characters that made up the cast of that early life so different from those among whom I live now, that they might just as well have lived five hundred years ago, rather than in the early twentieth century. The speed of change is such a cliché but when one delves into the past, as I have been doing, it does seem that the speed of change in the last century was so great that perhaps we have never quite caught up.

I suppose everyone finds his or her own life extraordinary, but my life has truly been lived in extraordinary times and in the context of extraordinary events. I think it must be unusual to have lived through the post-colonial and pre-apartheid days in South Africa, the Second World War, the horrors of the apartheid years, experiencing them at first hand, the years of UDI (Unilateral Declaration of Independence) in Rhodesia and, most amazing of all, to have that followed by a life working for some of the most prestigious arts organisations in the UK. Looking back I find it incredible and so unlikely that I sometimes wonder how it could possibly have happened. This memoir is a record of the facts as they occurred and, I hope, tells the tale and offers some explanation of how it all came about.

A DIVIDED WORLD

If it is believed that the early years of life influence it forever after, then it is essential to attempt to paint a picture of what life was like in the South Africa in which I grew up. This is probably for me the hardest task of all. I am obviously not attempting to write any sort of history of South Africa, or even to write about the whole complex situation; I am simply trying to describe the life into which I was born, how I saw it and how it affected me. And it really is difficult to give an accurate description of life in South Africa in those early days for someone who did not experience it, simply because it must come across as so unbelievable. To describe the years during which apartheid was actually the law is even more difficult. (Apartheid literally means 'separation'.) White South Africans lived lives of privilege and luxury, with a strong sense of entitlement, and most were entirely oblivious of the dark side of the shiny coin that was their life. Although the whites were surrounded and vastly outnumbered everywhere and every day by black people, the lives of the two races interacted only in a master–servant relationship. In a domestic setting that relationship could sometimes be very friendly, even intimate, and it was certainly so when black women, and sometimes black men, were trusted to care for the children of their employers. But we were the masters and they were the servants and that was that.

Generally, these white people were not monsters. They were ordinary people, in the main kindly and benevolent, living in circumstances they were born into, circumstances where there was simply no consciousness of black people as *people*. I realise that this was not always true. There were certainly circumstances where the employer might take a genuine interest in the servant's family, pay for a child to be taken to a doctor, bear the costs of school fees, listen carefully to stories of difficulty and offer help when it was needed. It was paternalistic, but at the time there didn't seem anything wrong with paternalism. I remember my husband being woken at 3 a.m. by our 'garden boy' knocking loudly on the door, very drunk, having fallen off his bicycle and scraped his face rather badly. He was quite unapologetic when my husband opened the door and he said simply, 'Plaster, please', confident that he would get the plaster and be treated kindly. I imagine he would have been very much in favour of paternalism.

In pre-Second World War South Africa, behind even the most modest of houses, there would be a separate building comprised of small, cell-like rooms and a lavatory. In an earlier period, there would have been no running water or electricity; later there was usually a shower, but seldom any hot water. It was in these buildings that the black domestic servants were housed. They were usually not allowed to have their families living time of an election, 'You must vote for Ian Smith – his father made the best sausages in Selukwe.' 'That's the only good reason I've ever heard for voting for him' was the reply.

I was born in January 1925 on a gold mine near a rather dismal little town called Benoni in the province of South Africa that used to be called the Transvaal and is now Gauteng. Births are often the result of unlikely meetings and unexpected coincidences and mine was no different. In my case it would not have happened at all if my forebears, on both sides of my family, had not been intrepid people who made the decision to move across the world to start new lives on different continents.

My father was Eugene Pomeroy Cowles and both the Cowles and Pomeroy families were from North America. He was born in Montreal in 1888. Tracing the families of both his parents I discovered that the Pomeroys (his mother's family) had been established for a considerable period before his birth in Compton in the province of Quebec; the Cowles family, his paternal family, were from New Hampshire and Vermont in the United States. Both families were English in origin and the Cowles, or at least some of them, I found – to my dismay – were Puritans and had left England in the eighteenth century. In the United States today this is considered rather a good thing but I am not very pleased; my mental picture of them is of stern-faced, stiff-necked, self-righteous bigots with a lot of facial hair. As far as I can gather, one branch of the descendants of these early arrivals in the United States moved to Canada sometime in the late eighteenth or very early nineteenth century and settled in the province of Quebec. It is very probable that they found themselves on the losing side in the American Civil War. It was here that my grandfather, Eugene Chase Cowles, the son of a doctor, was born and here, presumably, that he met my grandmother, Elizabeth Victor Pomeroy, who was one of a number of siblings, including three sisters, Elsie, Lucy and Mary.

Photography might not have been at its best at the time but photographs of the Pomeroy sisters and their mother reveal them all to have been extremely plain women – strong-faced certainly, but definitely plain, not a beauty or even a vaguely pretty face among them. They were all intellectuals. Mary was rather a good painter who actually managed to go to the Netherlands to study, which was quite an achievement for an unmarried young woman at that time, and Elsie wrote and published poetry. But it was my grandmother who was later to follow the most unusual and unconventional path. She became a Bahá'í, a member of a Middle Eastern religion that had originated in what was then Persia.

A more mismatched couple than my paternal grandparents, Eugene Chase Cowles and Elizabeth Pomeroy, could hardly be imagined. She was the plain blue-stocking, in love with him. He had a very good bass voice and was soon to embark on a career, with his wife's encouragement, as a professional singer. Thanks to the miracle of the computer and the internet, one can now hear recordings he made at the time. They are, of course, very scratchy and consequently sound horrible. He was also a composer of a vast number of popular songs, whole books of them. Sheet music was in great demand and he earned a lot of money. He sang with a company called the Bostonians and then joined the Alice Nielsen Opera Company, which toured to London and other European cities. At the height of his career, performing in New York and Boston and composing songs, he was very well known and successful.

My grandmother was proud of his talent and did everything she could to support his career, trailing around after him, by this time with a baby son in tow, in order to be present at all his concerts and opening nights. I doubt he was pleased by this reminder of his marital state as he had fallen in love with a member of the company. In defiance of all the accepted social conventions of the time and I think because she truly loved him, my grandmother agreed to his request for a divorce, leaving my poor father to be brought up by his mother, his grandmother and a bunch of spinster aunts – and living with the very real shame and social stigma of having divorced parents. My grandfather married for a second time and remained married to his second wife for over fifty years.

My father's grandmother and all her daughters lived in Montreal, where my father went to school. He had inherited his father's talent for singing but, apart from his years as a chorister in Montreal, he steadfastly refused to have his voice trained, as for him it was his father's musical career that had been the cause of all his childhood unhappiness. Fortunately he was clever, and funny, which I think can only have come from his father. He

My mother in 1934

top My mother and friends performing in an amateur musical
bottom left My grandmother, mother and aunt
bottom right My twin uncles, Cyril and Harold

top left Four generations of my father's family in Montreal
top right My grandfather, Eugene Cowles
bottom left My father, graduating from Montreal University
bottom right My father in uniform in 1917

Eugene Pomeroy Cowles, my father, in 1934

and an English couple named Villiers, who lived nearby, befriended the young family and took care of my grandmother while her mother was ill. After her mother's death, which followed not long afterwards, these good people approached my grandmother's young father and offered to adopt her. It is scarcely surprising that he agreed. I have no idea what became of him – he has disappeared into the blank pages of the past. There must have been memories, but I have no recollection of my grandmother ever sharing them.

In the early 1930s, some seventy years after their departure from Denmark, my grandmother's family went to extraordinary lengths to trace her whereabouts. In the days before Facebook and Google, I can't imagine how they achieved this, but they did, and in due course a letter, correctly addressed to her, arrived from Denmark. She no longer spoke Danish and the letter had to be translated. It is very frustrating that nobody knows what was in it. My grandmother told no one and, after reading the translation, she simply tore it up. It leaves the puzzle of why it was so important for them to find her. Now, I shall never know.

Her adoptive parents were very good to her and, when she grew up, they arranged for her to take a job as governess to the children of a wealthy sheep farmer in the Karoo. It was here that she met and married my grandfather. She was very beautiful with wonderful thick blond hair, the brightest blue eyes I've ever seen and a better sense of humour than anyone I have ever met. She was also someone of great dignity and reserve who, it would seem, did not welcome intimate friendships. Although I'm sure she was kind and I know she entertained a lot, she was probably not at all popular with most of the other women with whom she came into contact in that part of South Africa. I am sure they would have regarded her as 'stuck up'. She took absolutely no part in the informal social life of South Africans of that time and in those circumstances. She never approved of casual ways and she did *not* allow 'dropping in', which was very much the custom then in rural South Africa. She always maintained high standards in her dress and behaviour and expected everyone else to do the same. My mother told me that she once said, 'A woman should never come out of her boudoir until she is completely dressed' – so none of the cups of coffee in the kitchen, still in a dressing gown or just pyjamas, that is the way we live now. And I love the word 'boudoir'.

It would have all been rather forbidding if it were not for that sense of humour. I can remember her laughing until tears rolled down her face. She had nine children of whom six boys and two girls survived. My mother was the third child and grew up in a small town in the Karoo, which was the centre of enormous sheep farms, where my grandfather had a successful business. Surrounded by six lively brothers and one very quiet sister, family life was rowdy and boisterous and my mother seems to have been as boisterous and rowdy as any of her brothers. They all played highly competitive games – my mother told me that she was the best at marbles. They climbed trees, schooled untrained horses and appear to have been perfectly happy fighting among themselves. My grandmother did not approve of the local schools and all eight children were sent to boarding school, six in Cape Town and two to Grahamstown in the Eastern Cape. I was told that one of the boys, Lennox, was rather quieter than the rest of the family and all the children decided he was a changeling.

In thinking about these pioneer people from whom I am descended, both on the paternal and maternal side, people who almost three hundred years ago travelled from Europe to North America and from Europe to Africa in extremely arduous and dangerous circumstances, I am impressed by the quality of courage and the spirit of adventure that they must all have possessed. I long to know what made them do it. It doesn't seem that any of them were wanted by the police or were escaping desperate conditions of poverty at home. Yet they all made an unforced choice to emigrate.

CHILDHOOD

My father was working in Johannesburg. My mother had a pretty singing voice and had studied piano with a rather good teacher, a French woman in Cape Town, becoming quite accomplished. It was decided that, as there seemed to be nobody about that she wanted to marry and there was nothing to keep her in the little Karoo town, she should go to Johannesburg and keep house for one of her bachelor brothers, Reginald, who was always known as Reg. At the same time she would teach piano and singing to a few private pupils. This was very typical of the period. There was plenty of time for dances and tennis parties and it was an arrangement that suited both my mother and her brother Reg very well. Reg was later to marry Margaret White, one of the first female dentists to qualify at Edinburgh University. She did not have a private practice but was employed by the mine where Reg worked, looking after the teeth of the black miners. While my mother was there, Reg was still a bachelor. It was 1914; the possibility of a war in Europe that would affect both of them seems to have taken a long time to appear on their horizon. When it finally did, two of my uncles, Reg and Cyril, joined the Royal Flying Corps. Reg flew in those tiny aircraft tied up with string. Two more brothers saw action in what was then called German East Africa, which covered the area now divided between mainland Burundi, Rwanda and Tanzania.

My father was in a reserved occupation. On the outbreak of war, the company for which he worked informed him that he would have to stay where he was. This was met with a point-blank refusal. He handed in his resignation and applied to join the Royal Engineers in England. A week before he was due to leave, he met my mother at the house of mutual friends. I suppose it must have been love at first sight because before he left they became engaged and my mother always said that she 'just knew' that he was the person she was meant to marry. They were to be separated for the next four years and it says everything about my mother's nature that, despite other men wanting to marry her, she remained faithful to her promise to wait for him.

When my father left to go to England no one had any idea of what the future held, but like so many others he was about to enter hell on earth and undergo experiences that would change his life and almost certainly lead to his early death at the age of forty-six. Photographs of him taken at the time show a young man with dark, sunken eyes and a haunted face. He never ever talked about the war. My mother told me that he used sometimes to scream in his sleep. He was one of the tunnellers in France. Sebastian Faulks's novel *Birdsong*, later made into a film, gives some insight into what he will have gone through. By 1918 he was a captain in the Royal Engineers. He was very badly wounded in battle, losing his left arm and suffering severe wounds to his left leg. For his part in an earlier battle he was awarded the Military Cross. The citation in the *London Gazette* of 15 March 1918 reads:

For conspicuous gallantry and devotion to duty. He led his party forward with the attacking troops, and continued at his work of searching enemy dug-outs and cellars for over seventeen hours during a heavy and continuous bombardment and enemy counter-attacks. He assisted materially in the defence of the captured position and undoubtedly prevented many casualties.

After a period of recuperation, he was sent back to Canada on long leave and finally returned to South Africa in March 1919. I have some letters of his written to my mother at this time, many from the trenches, but in one of them, written during the recovery period in Canada, he says that he has spent the weekend with friends and that he was pleased by how well he could manage 'using my right hand and my teeth'.

My mother and he were married a week after he arrived back in South Africa in the little Anglican church in Kalk Bay and they started married life in Johannesburg, where he resumed his employment with the Union Corporation.

My brother Victor was born in December 1919 and a second boy, Peter, arrived two years later. This child was born with a digestive problem, one that could nowadays be treated easily and successfully, but he died at the age of six weeks on the operating table. My mother, who to her dying day regarded life as a running battle with the medical profession, always blamed the surgeon for his death.

Three years later, in 1925, I was born and Nanny entered our lives. Annie Purvis Ewart was from Keswick in Cumberland and had gone into service as a nursery maid at the age of thirteen, eventually becoming the head nurse in rather distinguished households. She was a tiny person and during her first years in service she had to carry loads of coal up flights of stairs, weights that were far too heavy for her young body. This resulted in various medical problems and considerable pain in later life. Nanny taught me all I was ever to know about poverty among the working classes of that time in the United Kingdom and her descriptions of her mother's battle to raise six children on a pittance are with me still. When she went out to work it was without question her duty to send the larger part of her wages home to help her mother. She taught me how afraid those in employment were of illness; falling ill almost certainly meant losing your job. It is very much with Annie

Purvis Ewart in mind that I appreciate the NHS and the safety net that exists now and didn't then.

In her last job before she left England she was nurse to the children of Stafford Cripps, a prominent Labour politician who was knighted in 1930. There is nothing I don't know about John, Theresa and Peggy. When Peggy Cripps married a prominent Ghanaian, in a blaze of publicity, Nanny was not at all pleased. I was interested to learn that the brilliant Professor Kwame Apiah, philosopher and writer, who teaches at New York University and gave the 2016 Reith Lectures, is the son of that marriage. After one of the lectures, in answer to a question as to whether he had suffered as he was growing up because of his colour, he replied, 'I was very protected. When I first went away to school my grandmother wrote to the headmaster and said, "If anything bad happens to my grandson, I'll have you killed!"' The extraordinary Lady Cripps, Nanny's employer, about whom I knew so much, caring for her grandson.

One of Nanny's sisters had married and her husband had taken a job in South Africa, uprooting his family. Homesick and lonely, her sister begged Nanny to join her, promising, 'There is plenty of work in this country.' Had Nanny not agreed I would not have been brought up by one of the most remarkable women I have ever known and the woman who, apart from being the most important influence in my life, was also the person I loved more than anyone else. But for poor Nanny it was a terrible decision – she made one brief visit to England, paid for by my father, but apart from that she remained in South Africa for the rest of her life, homesick all the time, yearning for the fells and the lakes and the flowers that formed the background to all the tales she told me as she gazed out at the dry, arid landscape of the Highveld. When she made that visit to England I was about three years old; it was not long after my grandmother's visit. Apparently the deal made at the start of her employment was that after the first three years she would be given a return ticket to England, and that if she then decided to remain there, that would be perfectly acceptable. Years later, knowing how homesick she had been all her life, I asked her why she came back to us. 'Because I had promised you,' she said.

So I grew up in the nursery, blissfully happy with Nanny. Victor, five years older, and not Nanny's baby, did not fare so well and was often on the receiving end of the rough edge of her tongue. But he was soon to go away to prep school and he played very little part in my early life. I do, however, have a very early memory of him constructing a sort of tent made out of rugs in the garden and persuading me to get into it so that he could undertake a detailed medical-type examination of my body. I remember rather enjoying it and being pleased by this unexpected attention.

I did not spend much time with my mother and infinitely preferred the nursery and Nanny. My mother always smelled very nice and her hands were smooth, which I liked, but she was often not very well and seemed to retire frequently to bed with headaches. 'Don't make a noise. Mummy is not well.' I adored my father but he was always either working or playing golf on Sunday mornings and I saw little of him. He would come into the nursery when I was having supper and to my astonishment sometimes, if I was having a boiled egg, would eat the shells, which I thought was very funny. I was always proud when he asked me to do something for him. One of my tasks was to fill his cigarette case; having only one hand made it difficult for him. I marvel now at the way he managed his disability and we were certainly not brought up with the idea that our father was in any way disabled. He could do everything one-handed: he drove a car, and they were not adapted in those days; he played golf; he could tie his own tie. In fact the only limitation I can remember was that my mother had to cut his fingernails. She told me that they had the perfect marriage but when I look back I sometimes wonder, just a little.

It has to be said that I was a very weird child. Had it not been for Nanny's good sense, I shudder to think what would have happened to me. When I was about five years old I started to stammer very badly. Nanny issued orders: 'Please don't mention Moira's stammer. Just ignore it.' And sure enough, after a while, quite a long while, it disappeared. Then there was the thing about being a boy. At about the same time as the stammer, I became more and more annoyed with the fact that I was a girl. I read nowadays about childhood 'gender confusion'. I certainly did not suffer from this; I knew perfectly well that I was a girl and I didn't like it. It was obvious to me that boys had a better time. In imaginary games I was always a boy but, to my intense frustration, there seemed to be no way of making it reality. I thought about this a great deal and considered how I might miraculously turn into a boy, but eventually I had to accept defeat. At least I could dress as a boy. So I begged for boys' clothes, proper boys' clothes, shorts with flies and boys' shirts and boys' school caps, and I steadfastly refused to wear dresses. Again Nanny showed understanding and sympathy and took me to the boys' departments in shops to buy clothes. She allowed no one to comment. 'She'll just grow out of it.' Thank God this was before the days of the child psychiatrist or, Heaven help us, gender re-assignment.

Because we lived on a mine away from any town, we were fairly isolated and I was a solitary child who lived in an imaginary world. I can't think now why I did not mix with the other children whose fathers worked on the mine, but I didn't. In my imaginary life, I was, of course, a boy and always a boy with many siblings, the eldest son of a very poor woman who expected me to help her survive. Perhaps this arose from Nanny's tales but this imaginary life I led was in many ways more real to me than my everyday life in the nursery. I longed to go to school (a boys' school) but at that time my only instruction came from Nanny. After breakfast, I used solemnly to say goodbye to her, walk around the garden and then knock at the door and reappear for 'school'. Nanny never failed me. 'Good morning,' she would say. At the end of my lessons, I would leave and then reappear to tell her all about the morning's classes. Poor Nanny. To her eternal credit she listened carefully, as though it was all new to her. She never read fiction and she had done her best to educate herself by reading all the books she could lay her hands on. Had she been educated, I could easily picture her as a politician, battling for the poor and underprivileged.

As if the boy thing was not enough, there was also my obsession with church. I had never been in a church and had absolutely no idea what happened in them. My parents were nominally Anglicans but religion didn't bother them much, if at all, and certainly no one in my family ever went to church. I used continually to ask my mother, but the answer was always, 'No, darling, you can't go to church. Daddy plays golf on Sunday mornings and it's Marshall's day off.' Marshall was our chauffeur. 'And, anyway, you'll get quite enough of that when you go to boarding school.' Although I can't now imagine why, I continued to yearn for church and, of course, I was deeply interested when a little girl who knew all about it came to stay with us. Her parents were friends of Nanny and she, although not a Catholic, was at a convent school. She told me all about the school chapel and the prayers, the candles and the incense. The more she told me, the more fascinating I found it, and the more I wanted it. Having carefully absorbed the details, after she left us I decided to build my own church being offered reasonably well-paid employment that would enable them to support their families and, at the same time, were being looked after very well.

My father was at the top of this hierarchical structure and we lived in an unreal world of extreme privilege and luxury with black servants to look after every need. Nanny was in an entirely different category and was part of the family, as was, to a lesser extent, the chauffeur, who, for some reason I don't know, was always a white man. Then there was the cook, usually a black man (although my mother had experimented with employing white women, who almost always turned out to be alcoholics; on one famous occasion one was roaring drunk just before the start of a dinner party), and three 'house boys' (adult black men) plus several gardeners, called 'garden boys'. Everything that we ate was fresh and produced at home; we had hens and ducks and cows as well as a well-stocked vegetable garden. There were stables where my brother had a horse and I had a Shetland pony. Poor Nanny had to be introduced to the purely South African food that we occasionally also ate. The great treat was the annual arrival of the penguin eggs that were ordered from a government department that controlled the sale of these delicious eggs; applicants were allowed two dozen per year. Larger than duck eggs, with translucent whites, they have a slightly fishy taste. Hard boiled with butter and salt and pepper, they are among the best things I've ever tasted. We also loved biltong, spiced, dried raw meat, which Nanny found disgusting.

So I grew up leading a strange and very solitary life. The only other children I ever saw were the children of the mine doctor and occasionally the children of other mine managers. The Bushells were the children of a manager of a neighbouring mine. Elizabeth was my contemporary and her brother Roger was later, during the Second World War, to achieve worldwide fame as the originator of the 'Great Escape' from Stalag Luft III in Lower Silesia; he was shot in the back with all the other recaptured escaped prisoners. Nanny sometimes took me to Johannesburg to spend time with the charges of her few friends, other English nannies out in South Africa to care for South African children. Nanny Webber was her great pal and on two occasions the two nannies, mine and Nanny Webber, set off on the long train journey to the seaside at the south coast of Natal with me and the two younger Webber children, Julian and Diana. Why we were sent off without our parents for these quite long holidays I have no idea, but we didn't mind at all and these times bring memories of pure pleasure. Even now I can see the grey, dusty path that took us to the beach from the thatched bungalows in which we were living, and smell the sea and see the lush, green, exotic foliage of the trees that surrounded the beach of fine white sand.

It was on one of these holidays to the seaside, but this time to the Cape, that Nanny took me to see Houdini perform. I can clearly remember standing on a street in Muizenberg, a seaside suburb of Cape Town, with hundreds of others, watching as a man was manacled and chained and put into what Nanny told me was a straitjacket, tied up further and then suspended from a sort of crane. In amazement we saw him escape from all the restraints and then climb down to a wooden platform. It was only decades later that I read that Houdini had been in Cape Town in 1929 and realised that he was the escapologist I had been taken to see.

When I was approaching my tenth birthday, it was decided that it was time to send me to school and I was dispatched to St Andrew's in Johannesburg as a boarder. I was very keen to go but when the time came, the shock to my system can hardly be described. Without any transition, I was pitch-forked from the sanctuary of the nursery into the unfamiliar and terrifying atmosphere of a girls' boarding school. Apart from Nanny's instruction in the three Rs and a little more advanced mathematics, which I had been taught by Mrs Edwards, a professor's daughter who had married an official at the mine, I had had no education whatsoever and had never even seen or imagined a classroom, let alone a dormitory. I can still remember my terror on that very first night, after the lights had been put out, when, through sheer nerves, I realised that I needed to go to the lavatory. How I managed to find it I can't remember, but I certainly can remember very clearly the fear I felt. This was when I started to want, desperately, to belong but I was very ill equipped to achieve it.

FAMILY CHANGES

St Andrew's was quite a happy school but from an academic point of view an appalling one. I am told it is much better now. For some unknown reason, the school employed only British women, as opposed to South Africans, and as a consequence we were taught by the rather sad spinster daughters of English vicars who, I suppose, thought that they might find husbands in South Africa. The calibre of teacher in England who wanted to work in Johannesburg between the two world wars was not of the highest. We did, in fact, have a good French teacher, who was herself French and I liked and admired our Latin teacher, but the rest were a pretty dismal lot. Games and sporting prowess were terribly important but I was a skinny, badly co-ordinated child and team games were torture and humiliation for me. I was always the last to be picked for the team.

I had to learn all the manners and traditions of the school, all of which were entirely unfamiliar to me. There was one that I find now to be quite surprising. If anyone had something, a book or a piece of clothing, a ball or almost anything that was unwanted she would lift it up and shout, 'Quis?' The person who replied 'Ego' first became the recipient. It seems quite strange that little white South African girls in a Johannesburg school in the mid-twentieth century should have had this tradition of shouting in Latin among themselves. Where did it come from, I wonder, and was it common perhaps in boys' schools in England?

I was to spend the next six years of my life at St Andrew's and by the time I was at the top of the school I was really quite happy, and confident enough to be rather badly behaved. My great friend Kathryn Reunert, the head girl and I (a prefect) took up smoking in our last year and used to smoke on a little hidden balcony every night after supper. Generally life was tolerable.

I went to school in January 1935 when I was ten years old and in July of that year my father died. I happened to be at home for what was called a 'going-out Sunday' when it was discovered that I had measles and consequently I was not sent back to school at the end of the day. On the Thursday of that week my father came to the nursery door to say goodbye to me and said, 'I'll see you at lunchtime.' He then went underground on an inspection and suffered a massive heart attack from which he died. Not much is said about the intensity of the grief children can suffer, but I remember the pain and the anguish only too clearly. It was sharpened by the fact that ours was an agnostic family and there was no one and no place to offer a shred of comfort. I longed to be able to talk to someone, to ask, 'Where is he now? What has happened to him?' But there was nobody. I remember that, in a sort of insanity and desperate for an answer, I thought that maybe if I wrote a letter and burned it, perhaps there would come some sort of answer from an other-worldly source. Of course, I knew that I was being silly.

My poor mother was devastated by my father's death and she was hopelessly ill prepared to deal with a new life and the upbringing of two children. She was brave and she did her very best but it was very hard for her; she had been so spoiled and protected all her life and suddenly the very foundations of her existence were gone. With his death, our lives were changed for ever and, in many ways, were never to recover. Not only was he, the rock on which it was all built, gone, but everything else too, the whole edifice – the house, the way of life, certainty, the privilege and, of course, the financial security. As he died at such a young age, his pension was not very large and the capital he had managed to acquire and invest was really not adequate. We moved to Johannesburg into a small house my mother bought. Nanny valiantly stayed on for a few years and my mother learned to drive. My brother Victor was fifteen and at boarding school in Natal. He was good looking, an exceptional sportsman, and was just beginning to realise that not only was he attractive to women but that his charm could carry him effortlessly through most of the challenges of life. He was also soon to be enchanted by the effects of alcohol and no teenage boy has ever been more in need of the firm discipline of a father. My mother, who had fallen in love with Victor when he first opened his eyes and simply adored him, was no match for the situation. Added to these problems were the expectations that surrounded him and which were encouraged by all my father's colleagues. He must follow in his father's footsteps and so poor Victor would, in due course, when he was only seventeen, be sent to Canada to read mining engineering at McGill University.

He was bright and had many talents but engineering was most certainly not one of them. The whole venture was a very expensive disaster. However, the Second World War broke out while he was in Canada and this saved him from further humiliation in the engineering department. He returned, not yet twenty, to join the South African Air Force. He became a very good pilot, I was told, and eventually he was sent to serve as a fighter pilot in the Middle East. When he returned home, there were, of course, lots of stories, some of which were very funny. My favourite was of his great friend, Philip Bryant, who had a sweet but rather unsophisticated mother. Philip, like most young men, needed a top-up to his available spending money, and he wrote to his mother, 'All the others here have parachutes. I really need one too, so could you possibly send me some money?'

Two years before the outbreak of war our new financial instability had been increased by a further disaster. One of my mother's six brothers, Harold, introduced her to a friend of his, the local manager of Barclays Bank, a man my uncle said was 'very good with money and investments'. He came to dinner and I took an instant dislike to him but unfortunately the opinion of a twelve-year-old girl was not likely to be taken into account. This man – all the time employed by Barclays – gradually took over my mother's affairs and persuaded her that it would all be much easier if he and my uncle had her joint power of attorney, so that he could immediately take advantage of 'tips' he had for investment on the stock exchange. My mother, like several other members of her family, was a born gambler – poker and horse racing were lifelong obsessions – and in the circumstances in which she had been left, the chance of increasing her capital was irresistible. And so my uncle and his friend signed documents on my mother's behalf for transactions that were designed purely to enrich my uncle's friend and which my uncle simply failed to read. 'Well, I trusted him,' he said afterwards. Perhaps the situation could have been saved but in 1937 the Johannesburg Stock Exchange crashed and almost everything we had was gone. My mother knew the general manager of Barclays socially and in a desperate attempt to obtain some sort of compensation she went to see him. Well, of course, she was told, there is quite enough here to put the man in gaol, but if you bring an action, I'm afraid your brother will go to gaol too. This was absolutely out of the question as far as she was concerned and that was the end of that. It was typical of her nature that my mother bore my uncle no grudge and I often wondered, in later years, whether he appreciated what she had done for him. I don't think so. Although he was a kind man, amusing and attractive in a way, he was quite stupid. I never thought much of him and my favourite uncle of all the six was his utterly different twin brother, Cyril.

This was a very difficult time and it was now that someone introduced my mother to Christian Science. She had always been something of a sucker for the occult; she loved fortune tellers and spiritualists and I think that she saw Christian Science in rather the same light. She started reading the book by Mary Baker Eddy and occasionally attended what, I think, were called Testimony Meetings in the Christian Science church. On one occasion she had a bad headache and asked me to fetch her some aspirin. 'Hang on,' I said. 'I thought you were a Christian Scientist.' 'Oh,' she replied, 'aspirin is quite different.' The whole experiment came to an end not long after.

By 1939 when the war started all this was behind us but we were still feeling its effects and my mother was permanently worried about money. I believe that a friend of my father offered to help with my school fees but my mother was far too proud to accept his offer. What made it especially hard for her was the fact that there had always been more than enough money. Her own father had been a rich man, albeit a gambler too, and inevitably, as my father's career advanced, they had lived a very comfortable life. Suddenly, here she was worried about paying bills; even as a child it used to worry and frighten me to find her weeping over a pile of unpaid accounts, knowing that she had absolutely no idea how to manage money. A few years afterwards she told me that she was selling some shares and I asked whether this was a good idea? 'Well, you can't live without money' was her characteristic response.

WAR IS DECLARED

These concerns were always there but in the background, and the start of the Second World War tended to sweep all other thoughts away. The beginning of the war was dramatic in South Africa. Although the country was still, after the Boer War, divided between English and Afrikaner, and Parliament reflected this division, it would be difficult to explain to an outsider how muddied the dividing lines were and yet how bitterly they were observed, especially by many of the Afrikaners. They hated the British, and the British, on the whole, just looked down on them. The opinions of the black majority were, of course, not considered.

There were the rather grand, old Afrikaner families, mainly Huguenot and very early settlers, who were totally absorbed into the 'English' – and what we thought of as the civilised – half of the country, and there were also Afrikaner intellectuals such as General Smuts who saw the future of the country as best served by relegating all these divisions to the past. But very many Afrikaners – led, it must be said, by some who were well educated – were poor and felt themselves dispossessed; they retained an almost pathological hatred of the British. It was these Afrikaners who won the election after the war and who led the country down the insane and tragic path of apartheid.

South Africa's entry into the war was bitterly opposed by the Nationalist/Afrikaner section of Parliament, who saw it as a 'British' war and it was due only to the skill of the prime minister, General Smuts, that the opposition was narrowly defeated and South Africa declared war on Germany. There was no conscription and every single South African who fought in the Second World War did so as a volunteer. Members of both the regular and the volunteer armies were told that they could abstain from service abroad and serve only in defence of their country if they wished. All volunteers who agreed to serve abroad wore a red flash on their uniforms and this soon became to us a sign of loyalty.

To begin with, and long before the battles of the Middle East in which South Africans were to fight with such distinction, the country, on the surface, was very little affected. Petrol rationing was introduced, fund-raising drives and initiatives to support the armed services were started and my brother and all his contemporaries joined the services. However, at the same time, the Broederbond, a secret Nationalist organisation that recruited only top, influential Afrikaners, and the Ossewabrandwag, a more open organisation, were both intent on undermining the war effort and giving help to the Nazis in whatever way they could – anything to make the hated British suffer. We were very aware of these people and saw them as traitors in our midst. The country was polarised and suspicion between the two sections of the white community increased.

I was only fifteen, soon to be sixteen, when I finished my school exams, and it was thought that I should complete a further year at school. However, I had passed my School Certificate with sufficient credits to go to university and had no desire to stay at school as all my friends, who were mostly older than I was, were leaving. My mother was by then very disenchanted with Johannesburg and decided that, as my brother was away in the Air Force, she and I would go and live in the Cape and I would go to Cape Town University.

I was far too immature and ill prepared to benefit from university but nevertheless, joined by a school friend, Lovelle Cullinan (the grand-daughter of the man who found the Cullinan diamond), who came to live with us, I entered Cape Town University, originally to read for a

BA degree. At that time this meant taking three subjects and mine were English, French and History. However, Lovelle took against the French professor, whom she loathed for some reason, and persuaded me to join her and change our course to Drama. Regrettably, education of any sort was very far from our minds and Drama turned out to be much more fun. We found ourselves studying with some rather strange girls and a few camp young men, who were either uninterested in or ineligible for military service. Plays, in which we had parts, were produced in the Little Theatre in Cape Town and generally life was very agreeable and study not at all taxing. Also studying there at the time was Leonard Schach, who went on to have such a distinguished career in the theatre in Israel.

After years in the strict confines of a girls' boarding school, it was only natural that our chief preoccupations were men and parties but we managed to fit in sufficient study to satisfy the authorities. (I was by then sixteen but my friends, Lovelle included, were all older and I always lied about my age, adding a couple of years.) I and all my friends might have been meant to be studying or, later, working and serving in the forces, but at this time having fun was uppermost in our minds. We knew lots of young South African men, there was always the Royal Navy stationed at Simonstown and, of course, the convoys, flotillas of troop ships guarded by the Royal Navy on their way to the Middle East and the Far East. Together these provided us with an endless round of parties and entertainment. For us there was the added delight of naval vessels going into Simonstown for re-fits, which might last for several weeks, providing perfect opportunities for enjoying ourselves. It was all harmless and, apart from the usual flirting, completely innocent. I'm sure that there were plenty of others who thought differently but among my little group of friends there was such a fear of becoming pregnant that sex was absolutely out of the question. These were the very early days and the tragic reality of war was to strike only later, when so many of these men with whom we had danced and laughed were killed or wounded or taken prisoner. Among the casualties, of course, were sometimes our own brothers and fathers.

South African hospitality during the war was legendary. Everybody opened their homes to the young soldiers, sailors and airmen passing through the Cape; they were invited to meals and, if they had a few days leave, to stay in South African houses as welcome guests. Kelvin Grove was the upmarket, exclusive country club, similar to those found so often in former British colonies, and with great generosity, all serving officers were offered membership of the club during their stay in the Cape. Not content with this, a well-known woman in Cape Town, Lucy Bean, undertook to arrange parties for officers if they were part of a convoy. These took the form of dances at Kelvin Grove to which, of course, they had free entry, and young girls who were considered 'suitable' were invited to meet and dance with the men – up to two or three hundred at a time. I met both Tom Curteis and Geoffrey Bennett, both of whom I was to marry (consecutively!), at Kelvin Grove.

My meeting with Geoffrey was totally by chance and became the subject later of a great many jokes. In Muizenberg, where my mother and I were living, there also lived a woman called Pearl Tankerville-Chamberlain, who seemed to me old and was, I suppose, about forty. Rather grand, she had fallen on hard times and was always trying to sell Lovelle and me her old clothes. She would telephone and say that a friend from New York, or Rio or San Francisco had had to leave behind some 'very beautiful clothes' and had asked Pearl to sell them for her. We became a bit wiser, but at first we would go and look at what were very obviously her own old things. Poor woman. And, as she had no car, she was always trying to cadge lifts. On this particular occasion, she telephoned and said, 'Moira, I was having lunch today with the Captain of HMS *Ramilles* and he has arranged a special party tonight for some of his officers. He asked me whether I would invite some nice young girls to meet them and I wonder whether you would like to go?' 'Yes, thank you, Mrs Chamberlain, I'd love it.' (I was now seventeen and had a driving licence.) 'Oh, that's good. Could you please give me a lift there?' Even I realised that that was the point of the invitation but I didn't mind and was happy to accept. The only snag was that when we got to Kelvin Grove, it was obvious that she had made the whole thing up. None of the officers in *Ramilles* had been invited and no party had been arranged. I doubt whether she even knew the Captain of *Ramilles*, but the ship was in Cape Town and there were a number of her officers present. I watched in astonishment, feeling terribly self-conscious and embarrassed, as she went around picking up young men absolutely unknown to her. 'I was having lunch with your captain today – would you like to join a party I've arranged?' Geoffrey was one of them.

This was in 1942. In December 1941, the day after the Japanese attack on Pearl Harbor, an event occurred that has always puzzled me. We, the 'suitable' girls, were invited to the usual party at Kelvin Grove and we were told that there would be many Americans present. Included in the party were lots of British army officers and a very considerable number of American naval officers. Of course, everyone was talking about the horrors of the previous day, when it was announced that General Smuts would be arriving and that he would make a speech. Suddenly the familiar and much loved white-bearded man arrived and in his thick accent talked about Pearl Harbor and what it meant to the world. He spoke warmly about the Americans, particularly those present, offering them a welcome to South Africa. Somewhat surprisingly and rather tactlessly I thought, he said, 'I have always wondered what contribution the Japanese have made to the world and now I know. They have brought the Americans into the war.' But it was a good speech and I'm sure it did much to cement South African–American relations, assuring those American naval officers present that their contribution to the cause for which we were all fighting was valued. But what continues to puzzle me about this event was that some of the British army officers to whom I spoke told me, perhaps indiscreetly, that they had been sent from Britain to Halifax in Canada and that there they were then transferred into American troopships manned by the American navy. This happened six weeks before they arrived in the Cape and thus six weeks before Pearl Harbor. Carrying British troops was obviously a breach of American neutrality and I can't help wondering how it was that, when this situation would necessarily become public, it just happened to be the day following Pearl Harbor and the United States was no longer a neutral state. I suppose we shall never know the answer but when I hear conspiracy theories, which always seem to me to be ridiculous, I remember this and wonder.

By now I had ceased to be a student at Cape Town University. Lovelle and I felt that it was wrong not to be playing an active role in the war and that being a student was unacceptable. Rather foolish of us, I realised later; I don't think that my efforts did much to bring about the downfall of Hitler but at the time we thought that to win the war required our efforts. Lovelle had already decided she wanted to join the services and had become a secret radar operator based on Robben Island, which sounded very appealing and adventurous to me. For three years she was stationed on the island, isolated and, of course, not permitted to discuss with anyone the nature of her work. Every three weeks or so she would be given leave and allowed to go to Cape Town but as this involved a journey in an unreliable little boat, leave was cancelled if the weather was bad. Her life was not the appealing adventure I imagined.

I didn't want to be left behind and another friend, Betty Wilks (later Parsons), decided that we, too, had to put our extremely limited abilities and talents into the war effort and we joined the WAS (Women's Army Services), where I had a very undistinguished career. Private Cowles, I was put to work every day from 8.30 until 5 extracting the information from a file and entering it onto a card. They called me a statistician. About three times a week, for some reason I never understood, we were required to march round and round a parade ground, stamping our feet and learning to left turn and right turn and shout out numbers. I was often in trouble because Betty insisted on being next to me and would hiss something out of the side of her mouth that made me laugh.

My mother had, since my early childhood, wanted me to be what she termed 'delicate' and, indeed, firmly believed that I was. This desire of hers had for one awful term plagued my school life when she had horribly embarrassed me by demanding that I receive special treatment, special food and special concessions which the school allowed only because the headmistress seemed to adore her. Added to this, for one whole term she removed me from school to spend the time on a farm in the Transkei to make me stronger. I pleaded with her and said that I would miss all the new work. She dismissed this: 'Rubbish, you'll soon catch up.' I have never understood her determination to turn me into this delicate creature, but determination it was. Obviously I wanted to be treated like everyone else; to belong was still very much my aim, but this was a point of view with which she had no sympathy. Nothing I said changed her mind.

Now, having got her way with school, she decided to take on the Army. I was not in barracks but living at home and so she was forever saying, 'It's ridiculous that you have to get up at this hour and take the train to Cape Town, all for some silly parade.' I rather agreed with her but, instead of my seeing it through, which was what I wanted to do, she did her best to persuade me that my time in the Army was not contributing anything to the war effort and that I could be doing something far more interesting. 'And anyway you are far too delicate for this.'

The author, aged twenty

Growing up in South Africa –
the author, aged four, eight and seventeen

He was with the partisans led by Tito for six months, moving by night and lying low during daylight hours. Although some were grateful for what he was doing, the partisan leadership was very prickly about its independence and resented having to rely in any way on outside help, particularly help from the British army, and they often made life very difficult for him. Of course, I knew none of this at the time, but I did know that he was engaged in something very secret for which he was later awarded the military MBE. He was out of touch for months at a time but, when they came, his letters continued to enthral me and I felt, absurdly, that I knew him really well. Oh, the glamour of someone doing such exciting, secret things!

In June 1944 the second front in Europe opened up; D-Day was 6 June. All the churches in Cape Town held services to pray for our troops taking part in the invasion and I, although not a churchgoer at the time, went to the service at the Anglican church in Claremont, a suburb of Cape Town. When I came out afterwards I saw a woman I knew, Anne de Nys, a very attractive and – in my eyes – immensely sophisticated person who was a singer and pianist who was well known in London as an entertainer but who had somehow got stuck in Cape Town during the war. She had a small girl with her, dressed in school uniform. I spoke to Anne for a short while and she introduced me to her sweet-looking child, 'This is my daughter, Virginia McKenna.' Recently I saw a television programme about Virginia McKenna revisiting Kenya and I sent her an email, telling her how we had met all those years ago and how attractive I thought her mother had been. She replied immediately and I think that my recollection had given her pleasure.

In early December 1944 Tom Curteis wrote to say that he was back in Italy and that he had asked for leave in South Africa. The reply from his Commanding Officer was that a secret document had to be delivered to South Africa, that he could take it to Pretoria but that he could have leave only if he was going to get married. A letter came saying, 'Darling Moira, will you marry me?' How could I possibly have refused? I was very young, nineteen, stupid, and naive. It all seemed so terribly exciting and romantic. The fact that I really did not know this man hardly entered my thoughts. Perhaps in my defence it could be said that the atmosphere in wartime was strange and unreal; people were doing unlikely things all the time. I was under twenty-one and I had to have my mother's permission to marry. Years later I asked her why she had given her consent and she said, 'I was frightened that he might go back to the war and be killed and that you would never forgive me.'

Tom flew to Johannesburg en route to Cape Town and was met there by my brother. Victor telephoned me after meeting him and said, 'For God's sake don't marry this man – he's very nice but he's bomb happy.' A truer word was never uttered. Poor Tom, what he had been through had really taken its toll, but, of course, Victor's judgement merely infuriated me. Tom flew to Cape Town on leave for two weeks. A wedding and a very small reception were hastily arranged with my poor mother in a state of shock. It says much for the generosity of her nature that she did everything possible to make it a happy and successful occasion. We were married in the Anglican church in Kalk Bay, the same church where my parents had been married, which for me made it all seem even more like a fairy tale. I can hardly believe now that anyone could be quite so unrealistic and, indeed, irresponsible as to marry a man that she knew as little as I knew Tom, but then I look at my grandchildren and great grandchildren and think that perhaps it was one of the best things I ever did.

AN ADMIRALTY CIVILIAN

Tom returned to Italy to whatever new and dangerous duties we had no idea, and the plan was for me to try to get to England as soon as possible and by whatever means. I had left my job with Naval Intelligence because I was going to be married and Stuart Bennett, whom of course I knew, stepped in and arranged my passage to England, travelling as an Admiralty Civilian. Shortly before I was due to embark I discovered that I was pregnant. This was definitely not part of my plan for the immediate future.

I felt nauseous most of the time and fainted rather often but nevertheless I found myself boarding a converted liner, crammed to the gunwales, carrying literally thousands of RAF personnel and about a hundred civilians. Among the civilians were my friends Betty and Billy Ward Jackson, both journalists, returning to London to take up posts in the newspaper world and accompanied by their baby son Nicholas. Their friendship and support on this awful journey were lifesaving.

There were six of us women in what had been a first-class cabin originally intended for two persons now with six bunks and one basin.

I must have been a great irritation as I felt so ill and still occasionally fainted, but on the whole my fellow passengers were kind. On our first day at sea we had lifeboat drill and everyone was ordered to be on deck at a certain time to practise getting into lifeboats. I fainted (yet again) and had to be scooped up off the deck. Lifeboat drill continued throughout the journey and we were told to have with us at all times one very small bag in which we had to have our most important possessions, including, of course, our passports. I kept changing my mind about what were my most important possessions, which was a worry, but after the second drill I decided that it was perfectly obvious that there were not enough lifeboats for all the hundreds on board and that I would go down with the ship rather than partake in a hideous scramble to get into one.

At that period of the war, ships carrying troops or civilians either went very slowly in a convoy protected by naval vessels or went alone, as fast as possible, hoping that the speed would be sufficient to protect the ship from enemy submarines. Our ship was on its own and went incredibly fast. We travelled from Cape Town to Liverpool in fourteen days, which was almost incredible at the time, particularly as our route took us out a long way to the west and then a long way to the north, all in an effort to escape detection by U-boats. Having gone far out west and before going north, we turned east and arrived in Freetown for one day. Here we were joined by the Freetown admiral's forbidding-looking wife, who was returning to England. The Ward Jacksons remarked that now we would really be in danger as the admiral was possibly anxious to be rid of her. For the rest of the journey to Liverpool we were escorted by two destroyers of the Royal Navy but really all I remember about this part of the voyage is the truly ferocious sea. We sailed into very rough weather and I could not believe that the waves breaking on the decks could be the height of tall buildings. It was the North Atlantic at its most fearsome and it was quite a frightening experience.

Eventually one early morning we docked in Liverpool, my first sight of Europe. To say that the view was dismal would be an understatement. It was grey and raining and I had never before seen hundreds of houses all tightly packed together in little rows. I found it quite a shock: most unlike Nanny's tales of the mountains and lakes and life in London in her employers' grand houses. We were met by the Women's Voluntary Service (WVS) when we disembarked. They gave us cups of tea and, in some misguided act of charity, we were given extra clothing coupons, in addition to the ration we were entitled to as new arrivals. Goodness knows where they thought we had come from. No one arriving from South Africa at that time was in need of extra clothing coupons and I was rather ashamed by this extraordinary generosity.

I was also a bit scared. It all looked, and indeed was, so unfamiliar and I really had no idea where I was going. I didn't know Tom well, and I certainly didn't know much about his family, with whom I was going to live. I had been instructed to send a telegram to his brother Bill, who lived in London with his wife Sheila. Bill was not in the services because he worked for the BBC French service. Tom had told me Bill would meet me off the train. We were allowed to send only one telegram and given strict instructions not to identify the ship we had been in or how long the voyage had taken. I sent the telegram to Bill Curteis and then, with hundreds of others, but feeling very alone, I boarded the train to London, hoping rather desperately that someone would meet me and my luggage when I got there.

LONDON AND SUSSEX

My arrival in London is burnt into my memory. I got off the train at Euston late on a rainy afternoon, managed to collect my luggage, and then stood there while everyone else around me was met with hugs and kisses and taken away. And there I stood. I did begin to feel panicky as I had only one lifeline and it wasn't there. Eventually, after what seemed rather a long time, a strange man came into view (it was foggy in my memory) and said, 'I'm looking for Mrs Curteis.' My relief can hardly be imagined. 'I'm Desmond Ryan. Bill Curteis is away but he has asked me to meet you.'

We got into a taxi and drove to Lincoln Street in Chelsea, to Bill's house which, of course, was empty. All I can remember is that I was very tired and very confused. I discovered later that Desmond was a rather distinguished literary figure but I did not know that then; nor did I know that he was also an alcoholic, a serious alcoholic, and that although when he met me he was charming and courteous, he was also drunk. He said that he and his wife would come back later and take me out to dinner. I have absolutely no recollection of the dinner but I do remember that

time, hampered slightly by my pregnancy and scared by the whole idea of having a baby.

In August the Japanese were defeated. Tom came home, now out of the Army, on 10 September, and on the 13th David was born in a small private maternity home in Henfield owned and run by the redoubtable Sister Balls. All I can remember of the experience is that while we were in the home David cried a lot and that I didn't know what to do. There were so many conflicting and confusing orders. 'Don't pick a baby up every time it cries'; 'Pick up the baby if you think it needs changing' – or is hungry or whatever . . . I was not naturally maternal and poor David must have suffered greatly from my incompetence. I wanted to cry as much as he did. I came in for a lot of criticism from my mother-in-law – she did not approve of the name David – 'It's not a Curteis name' – and she very much resented the fact that Tom used to walk to Henfield to spend time with me in the nursing home, when she wanted him at home with her.

After about ten days we went home to Gratwicks. When Tom's mother saw quite how incompetent I was I'm surprised that she didn't send for the Social Services, but luckily we didn't have them in those days.

When David was two months old, I was very ill with jaundice. The doctor reported the case and the local authorities arrived to carry out their examination. They discovered that we were all drinking well water (fortunately David's was boiled) and at the bottom of the well there were dead rats. I thought longingly of Africa where we drank tap water that came out of pipes. It took a while before I was fully recovered and then the great problem arose: 'What is Tom going to do?' As no one seemed to have any money it was borne in on him that getting a job would be a good idea, but it became clear that he really didn't know how to do this or what he wanted to do anyway. (Before the war he had been a professional soldier, left the Army and drifted about in Canada until war broke out and he returned to England.) He seemed quite resentful of the fact that he needed to work at all and I felt desperate. My mother-in-law said, rather grandly, 'I'm afraid we can't help as we just don't know anyone in business.'

I really didn't want to go back to South Africa but we, less grandly, did know people in business and I knew that Tom would be able to get a job there. I remember my mother-in-law saying, 'It's no good, Moira, taking Englishmen to those places as they are never happy.' 'Those places' meant what were still, to her, the colonies. In any event, as Tom was unable to make a decision I came to the conclusion that we had to go back to South Africa and I set about trying to arrange a passage, which was difficult in 1946.

TROUT FARMING IN AFRICA

I discovered that there were more or less normal passenger boats sailing between Lisbon and Lourenço Marques in Mozambique, then a Portuguese colony. What was missing in the equation was how to get to Lisbon. After endless enquiries and a great deal of nagging, we were finally booked on SS *Mouzinho*. We had a flight booked in a commercial plane, a recently converted bomber, from London to Lisbon. Looking back I think how mad it was, but we flew to Lisbon, accompanied by huge boxes of baby food and huge amounts of luggage, mainly for David's requirements, seen off by my tearful and disapproving mother-in-law. We spent three days in a hotel in central Lisbon and found that the shipping line refused to give us the sailing date; they told us that we had to come back every day and ask, and that on one miraculous day they would tell us when we were leaving. Very Portuguese, I discovered. The fact that we were paying passengers cut no ice at all. It was the first of our many unhappy experiences with Portuguese bureaucracy, and in particular with the marine authority. Finally we sailed with poor little David, six months old and very confused and out of sorts with all the changes and the lack of routine.

The voyage to start with was not too bad although I found very depressing the sight of the huge holds filled with wretched humanity in row after row of bunks stacked from the floor to the ceiling, sailing to Africa and the Portuguese colonies for the chance to start new lives. The Portuguese were enthusiastic colonists, and we seemed to stop at every single colony they had ever founded, places I had never even known existed – one, rather surprisingly to me, at the mouth of the Congo. We toiled along, very, very slowly, on what seemed like a never-ending voyage. Again the lack of information was maddening, and despite endless questions, the purser refused to give us a date for arrival in Mozambique. We stopped at Luanda where, to my astonishment, we refuelled. All portholes were shut and night and day African men ran up and down rope ladders with bags of coal; this was after all a steam ship and I hadn't given much thought to what would make the steam. Despite the port-holes being shut there was coal dust everywhere, and with the heat and the lack of fresh air, it was not a pleasant experience.

Our next stop was Lobito Bay and I was looking out of the port-hole as the ship was manoeuvred in to the dock. We seemed to be heading straight for the land and then with a sickening crunch we did, in fact, hit Africa, tearing an enormous hole out of the bows of the ship. Over the following three days I watched them filling the hole with concrete and then off we went again in very heavy seas. I remembered that the Cape of Good Hope was originally called the Cape of Storms.

The good thing was that the ship was ordered into dry dock in Cape Town, which meant that we could disembark there and that we did not have to travel all the extra way around the South African coast to Mozambique. The hateful purser made an unsuccessful attempt to force us, and all the others who wished to disembark, to pay the dock dues, a considerable sum of money, and did actually collect it from us, as we felt that we had no option but to comply. As soon as we arrived in Cape Town, we told the South African authorities, who came on board and, to my immense satisfaction, the purser was ordered to pay it all back.

We flew to Johannesburg and stayed with the incredibly kind Susskinds, the parents of a great friend of mine, Diney. She was in London at the time and I missed her, but her sister Pam, who was married to John Fordyce, a young naval officer, was there with her son, born a week before David. (Peter Susskind, Diney's brother, whom we all loved, had been killed at the battle of El Alamein.) Tom had accepted a job offered to him by Roly Cullinan, my friend Lovelle's father, to manage his trout farm in the Eastern Transvaal, and so after about three weeks we set out for Dullstroom and the farm in the Eastern Transvaal.

It was all a bit silly. Tom had not the slightest experience or knowledge of any sort of farming, let alone trout farming in Africa, which was a fairly new idea in 1946 and particularly in South Africa. We were heading for a traditional Afrikaner area, where English was not spoken and when it was, it was met with hostility. Neither Tom nor I could speak Afrikaans. If Tom did not know the first thing about farming, it was also a fact that I was unsuited in every way to farm life anywhere, let alone the Eastern Transvaal. And there was David. We had no neighbours; there was no other farm for dozens of miles, and there was no one to ask for advice. I was still a rather panic-stricken mother and on one never-to-be-forgotten occasion our poor child came down with fly-borne gastro-enteritis and had to be taken to a hospital forty miles away over rough, difficult dirt roads.

We employed a young black boy, aged about fourteen, to do odd jobs in the house. He was very bright and very nice but had had absolutely no education. He was delighted with the offer of work and was simply overjoyed when I bought him uniform clothes of white shorts and white shirts with a red binding. He wore the clothes with great pride until one appalling day when he came to me very subdued and frightened and said that he could no longer wear his uniform and that he would have to leave. When I asked for the reason he said that a local Afrikaner farmer had stopped him as he was walking along the road and said, 'Don't you dare to wear Englishmen's clothes. If you do I'll beat you first and then your flesh will rot off your bones.' This tale illustrates precisely the extent of the hatred that still existed in the rural areas among a proud, stiff-necked people who saw themselves defeated and humiliated by the hateful English.

We survived it for eight months and I said later that it was such an awful experience that nothing that happened afterwards could ever be worse. I am sure that Roly Cullinan was just as pleased to see us go as we were to leave. I had been left a very small sum of money by my father and with this we bought a house in Johannesburg and Tom set about trying to get a job. Family connections helped again and very close friends and relatives of my family who owned a publishing company, the CNA, arranged for him to see Adrian Berrill, the managing director. Adrian offered Tom the newly created job of personnel manager. Tom didn't know any more about personnel management than he did about trout farming but he, and presumably Adrian, thought that his experience of leadership as an Army officer should see him through any problems. And it must have worked because he was to stay in the company for years and for long after I had gone my separate way. It seems incredible now to think of the casual and uncomplicated way in which these things worked – the old boys' network in action.

APARTHEID

Almost coincidentally with our move to Johannesburg came the shattering result of the 1948 General Election when the very Afrikaners who had

they seemed not only blind to the obvious flaws in their vision of the future but completely oblivious to any moral or ethical considerations and to the horrific cost that ordinary people would pay. I suppose that in some small way they were better than the Nazis in that they did not have plans to obliterate an entire people; instead they intended to keep 'the blacks' alive to work for them. To hear the politicians, our rulers, talk about the virtues of apartheid and its Bible-based, God-given authority, in which some of them truly believed, was nauseating. Looking back, what amazes me is that otherwise rational people could possibly have imagined that they could separate two races, living in the same country *for ever*.

Almost immediately the Afrikaner leaders came up against a problem that, it seemed, had not occurred to anybody. 'We are going to establish a country where white and black will live separately. Black people can (of course) continue to work for white people but they will *live* separately and because we are good, God-fearing men we will give these lucky black people areas that we will call homelands. They may be hundreds of miles away from where they are now living, but we will send them there so that they can make homes and live peacefully miles away from white people.' Ah, but what shall we do about all those who are not completely black or not completely white but a bit of both?

There has always been in the Cape Province a group of people called Cape Coloureds. They are of mixed race and can trace their existence back to the very first Dutch settlers who came to South Africa in the seventeenth century. These people had always lived in their own areas, had developed their own culture and had always been recognised and respected as a separate people. The government certainly knew what to do with them. Their communities had always been close to white towns and cities and their culture was entirely white and Western but over a period of time the government bulldozed their houses, put them and their belongings onto lorries and moved them to bleak, barren land, where they could present no threat to white people. District 6, which had been an integral part of Cape Town, is a famous example of this racial cleansing; as is Sophiatown in Johannesburg where black people had always lived and where they actually had property rights. Both were emptied and bulldozed.

The real problem for the apartheid enthusiasts were the thousands who did not fit obviously into any category. Their *Alice in Wonderland* solution was to categorise all those not clearly black or white by examining them physically. So you might be ordered to attend one of these sessions in order that your fingernails could be examined – those with black blood have a slightly mauvish tinge, apparently. And, of course, your hair – how curly were the roots? These examinations were carried out by young, often poorly educated Afrikaners and at the end of it, after all the humiliation, you were categorised either black, white or coloured. One heard tragic stories, once of a young man pleading with his examiner, 'Please don't say I'm white. I'm married to a black woman.'

It is worth quoting from a piece that appeared in the South African publication *Business Day*, written some time after these regulations were brought in but when their application was in full force.

> Home Affairs Minister Stoffel Botha has told Parliament that last year 9 whites were re-classified coloured and 506 coloureds became white. 2 whites became Malay, 14 Malays became white, 9 Indians became white, 7 Chinese became white, 40 coloureds became black, 666 blacks became coloured, 87 coloureds became Indian, 67 Indians became coloured, 50 Malays became Indian, 4 coloureds became Griquas and 2 Griquas became black. No blacks applied to become white. 18 blacks became Griqua, 12 coloureds became Chinese, 10 blacks became Indians, 2 blacks became Malay, 5 blacks became other Asian, 2 other coloureds became Indian and 1 other coloured became black.

(Griquas and Malays are sub-groups of the Cape Coloured population. As though there were not enough black people to perform every possible kind of work, in earlier times, Indians had been imported to work on the sugarcane fields in Natal and Malays were imported by the early Dutch settlers from their colonies in Asia.)

Black and sex were somehow tied up in the imaginations of our leaders and miscegenation was their greatest fear. So great was this fear that it became illegal for a white man to be alone with a black woman anywhere but especially not in a car, with the consequence that if, for instance, a black female servant had missed her bus, her white male employer was not allowed to help by driving her home. It was against the law. Black chauffeurs were allowed to drive a white woman alone in the car and I can't now remember the details of what made this permissible; it was probably all right if the driver wore a uniform.

Many people have written about the evils of apartheid far better and more knowledgeably than I could. I simply want to show the backdrop against which we led our lives. All South Africans tend to be interested in politics but during these years it became, quite rightly I think, an almost obsessive interest. My own brother Victor, probably the least political person in the world, joined an organisation called the Torch Commando. These young men, often armed with a bar of soap wrapped in a sock hidden in a pocket, attended political meetings with the sole intention of ensuring that our opposition speakers got a hearing and were not prevented from speaking by a bunch of Afrikaner thugs. And years later my mother joined the Black Sash movement and, although well into her sixties, took her turn to stand silently outside government buildings in Cape Town.

Brave dissidents did much more and there were many arrests and the torture of black and white prisoners alike, but we ordinary South Africans simply did what we could and lived with shame and revulsion at what was being done in our name in our country. One young doctor was arrested and tortured for over sixty hours on end, resulting in his death in a police cell. And many anti-apartheid activists were served with banning orders that greatly restricted their freedom of movement. Dissidents were placed under house arrest and some were deported. I personally was not one of these courageous people and lived my life under the shadow of apartheid, doing nothing more active than voting against the National Party in elections.

I remember very well an instance, much later, when Julian – my youngest son – was a small boy, probably about four, and he and I were walking along the rocks at the end of Muizenberg beach. We heard cries and came across a young coloured couple. The man was fishing and he had cut himself badly with his very sharp fishing knife. There was blood everywhere and the young woman was panic-stricken. I told them to come as quickly as possible with me and that I would drive them to the nearest hospital which was in Fish Hoek, a small town nearby. We all got into the car, blood everywhere and I remember with shame how astonished they were that I, a white woman, would help them. I also remember Julian, a small boy on the same beach, looking at the notice reading WHITES ONLY. 'Does that mean that black people can't come on to this beach?' he asked. 'Yes.' 'But what if they can't read?' Which I thought was rather a good question.

In the first days of apartheid, as long as heads were deeply buried in the sand, life continued in its normal South African way. With a few notable exceptions, money was the only god anyone thought worth worshipping and among the white population a person's value was strictly and exactly measured by his wealth. Life was very brittle, envy and greed seemed to contaminate everyone and the really terrible thing is that we didn't know we were being contaminated, because life was fun and there was always another party to go to. The climate in Johannesburg is probably the best in the world and, while the houses are not particularly beautiful, the gardens are, not surprisingly, ravishing with smooth green lawns which the 'garden boy' tends and waters, and as long as the 'house boy', dressed in white uniform, was there to bring the drinks tray out on to the verandah at 6 p.m. there really was nothing to worry about.

Entertaining was lavish and featured very heavily in the lives of the privileged white people in Johannesburg, with tennis parties, cocktail parties and dinner parties the favourite ways of dispensing hospitality. At both cocktail parties and dinner parties, black servants were dressed for the occasion, wearing white suits, sometimes with coloured and tasselled sashes and even white gloves. I don't think that any of them saw this as any sort of indignity; rather, they enjoyed dressing up and there was competition between them as to which 'madam' gave them the smartest uniforms. At one of these dinner parties a visiting titled Englishman was being entertained – a feather in the cap of the hostess. On this occasion she rather forgot her lines and was heard to say to the black waiter, 'Give the Lord some more potatoes.'

Just at the time that the war had ended a great scandal erupted, rocking Johannesburg society. As in Cape Town, during the war, there had been a great deal of entertaining, and visiting soldiers and airmen were welcomed most warmly and looked after with great generosity. One of these was a young Air Force officer called Jimmy Armstrong, who was both handsome and charming. Before long he was a regular guest at all the best parties. He met a young woman I had always known, although we had not been at the same school. Poor Liz met Jimmy Armstrong, fell in love with him and shortly afterwards they were married in great style. Although he had a perfect explanation, people were rather surprised to find that he was now not in the RAF but had become an officer in the South African Air Force.

He was posted to one of the SAAF training stations and he and Liz occupied SAAF officers' accommodation. Some friends of mine went to spend a weekend with them and reported that all seemed very well, except that Liz had complained about the way Jimmy was carving the roast beef and, exasperated, he picked up the whole thing and threw it at her. They were not at this particular training station for long as Jimmy was transferred to another and promoted at the same time. It was here that Liz gave birth to their son Robert and not very long afterwards left Jimmy as the marriage had broken down. A divorce followed and Liz returned to live in Johannesburg with her parents.

As the war was ending Jimmy Armstrong was promoted once again and it was a promotion too far: the South African authorities discovered that Jimmy Armstrong was not Jimmy Armstrong at all but Neville George Clevely Heath. There were very red faces all around. How he had managed to be treated as a paid serving officer, entitled to accommodation and deserving of promotion by the SAAF authorities, no one seemed to know. The prime minister, General Smuts, was consulted. Instead of arresting him and making him face the music, however embarrassing that might be, it was decided to get rid of him as quickly as possible. He was put on a ship and sent to England where he embarked on his famous murderous spree, killing two young women on the south coast in a horrifying and brutal way. Heath was hanged in 1947. His son Robert was given another name and he and his cousins were regular playmates of my children. He grew up to be a very nice, rather ordinary, man with a nice wife and two children.

A NEW LIFE IN RHODESIA

Tom and I were not among the rich but we belonged in that milieu because I had been brought up in it in Johannesburg and we knew all the 'right' people. This, of course, was the worst of all possible worlds. It is not a part of this story to detail the ways in which we were affected, nor the ways in which we reacted to unhappiness, but the fact is that despite the birth of two further children, our daughter Nickie in 1948 and son Bill in 1951, the end of our marriage seemed inevitable and in 1953 we separated. Tom remarried not very long afterwards and, despite his mother's fears, remained in South Africa for the rest of his life.

I left with the children and went to the Cape to live for a while with my mother and then we all went to Salisbury in Southern Rhodesia (now Harare, Zimbabwe) and Geoffrey Bennett and I were married. He had been living in London after the war and went to Rhodesia for a long holiday during which he came down to Johannesburg and we renewed our friendship. Life in Salisbury in those days was rather like a pale carbon copy of the life I had led in Johannesburg: cocktail parties, tennis parties, lunch parties, all familiar to me but, understandably, not really to Geoffrey who, apart from seven years in the Navy, had led his entire life in London. Our marriage was a good one but the reality is that neither of us enjoyed Rhodesian life as it was then. I suppose it would have been very different if one was farming, but normal existence in Salisbury was stultifying and suburban with everybody talking endlessly about everybody else and seeming to have absolutely no other interests, except, perhaps, gardening. It was the ultimate ex-pat life; there was, of course, a certain amount of humour but irony was absent. An illustration of this, which was appreciated by some, was the story of the bishop's wife. The official residence of the Bishop of Mashonaland, then Bishop Paget, was set on a small hill, known locally as a *kopje* (pronounced 'copy') and was called Bishop's Mount. When Mrs Paget answered the telephone she always said, 'Elizabeth Paget, Bishop's Mount.'

One huge bonus for me was that my great friend Lovelle Cullinan, now married to Mervyn Hamilton, was living in Rhodesia and so were Tony and Jenny Upfill-Brown, old friends from Johannesburg. We made many new friends and these included Stewart and Betty Dismorr who had a house very close to ours; in fact, we lived in a cul-de-sac and their rather lovely Spanish-style house was at the very end of the road, closing it off from traffic. Nickie and Bill were at a day school at the time and used to cycle there, riding through the Dismorrs' garden, with permission, which saved them a considerable distance.

The Dismorrs were taking a long holiday and arranged to let their house, but Betty assured me that she had got the tenant's permission for the children to continue to ride through the garden.

However, quite soon Nickie and Bill told me that the woman renting the house had told them in no uncertain terms that they were never to go through the property again. They were furious but, of course, I told them that they had to observe her ruling. Shortly afterwards we began to notice that there was an enormous increase in the number of cars going along the road that ended at the Dismorrs' house. 'Why on earth are all those cars going to the Dismorr house?' we asked and the answer proved to be astonishing.

The tenants were charged with running a brothel. *A brothel? In the Dismorrs' house?* Stewart was a well-known ophthalmologist and a more respectable pair it would have been hard to find. More salacious detail was to be divulged. Mr Sen (never called anything but 'Mr Sen') was Swiss and working in Rhodesia as the representative of the International Red Cross. He and the Dismorrs were very friendly and he always stayed with them when in Salisbury; in fact one of the guest bedrooms was known as 'Mr Sen's room'. It now transpired that the brothel keepers had drilled a hole in the ceiling of Mr Sen's bedroom and inserted a camera in it. The customers were photographed at times that were very inconvenient for them and subsequently blackmailed. It was one of those being blackmailed who decided to go to the police. In the rather boring, suburban atmosphere of Salisbury, these revelations provided us with endless entertainment. Not quite so funny for the Dismorrs, who were furious and embarrassed.

Mr Sen became our friend too, and often joined us for Sunday lunch. I remember my surprise when he said one day, in answer to a question from me, 'Rhodesia is exactly like the Soviet Union. Here you have black and white. White people have all the privileges and black people none. In the Soviet Union party members have all the privileges and non-party members none.'

One day over lunch he asked us whether we would befriend a young black student at the university. (Black students were able to study at the new university.) Tranos Makombe, he said, was a very bright young black man who had never had the opportunity to meet and know a white family. Would we invite him to dinner? This was pretty well unheard of in the Rhodesian climate of the time, but we duly invited Tranos and Geoffrey drove to the university to fetch him for dinner. I will never forget the look of astonishment on the servants' faces when they saw him seated at our table as a guest.

The conversation was incredibly boring. There was really no meeting point and none of us knew what to talk about. Politics was obviously a touchy subject and so we laboured on trying to think of something to say. Geoffrey drove him back to the university and Tranos had obviously not been as bored as we were, as he asked whether we would invite him again. And so the whole exercise was repeated. Then he asked whether we would include his fiancée in the invitation. She was a nurse at the hospital for black people, some distance from the centre of town. Geoffrey drove to the hospital first and then to the university and did the whole thing in reverse at the end of the evening.

I decided we had done our bit and said to Geoffrey, 'This is ridiculous. You have to drive for miles and miles before we have dinner and then drive for miles and miles afterwards and, anyway, I don't think that anyone really enjoys it. I don't think that it is doing any good to anyone. We don't know what to talk about and conversation is so stilted.' He agreed and I thought that that was the end of it and that we would possibly not see Tranos again. Of course, we knew that one day there would be a black government and I thought that he would probably be a leading light in some future regime and that if heads were going to be chopped off, perhaps he would spare ours.

I was wrong. (I don't mean about the heads.) A short while afterwards a very correct, white-card wedding invitation arrived. Elizabeth and Tranos were to be married in the black area of Salisbury and we were invited. Geoffrey was going to be away, but we felt that we absolutely had to accept the invitation and so I asked David, now aged about sixteen, whether he would accompany me. It must be remembered that, although this was not apartheid South Africa, there was absolutely no social meeting between blacks and whites and our friendship with Tranos was quite exceptional.

The wedding reception was one of the most surreal experiences I have ever had. We arrived at the hall in the black township to find, unsurprisingly, that the guests were all black, except for a very small coterie of well-known liberals from the university. There were *lots* of speeches, many of them overtly political and looking forward to the days of black liberation – the public expression of such ideas was very much against the law. Then Tranos and Elizabeth, dressed in traditional white, opened the dancing with a slow waltz. It looked unusual to say the least. By now the number of guests had suddenly increased; they were pouring in through the open doors and the dancing took on a new dimension. No modern disco could have rivalled it.

We were sitting on chairs at the side of the dancing and unexpectedly a young black man seized David's hands and told him that he should be dancing. I had no idea how he would react but he greeted the invitation with enthusiasm, tore off his jacket and tie and hurled himself into the turmoil on the dance floor. Afterwards he said, 'I just hope that nobody at school ever knows about that.' We never did see Tranos again, as he left Salisbury, and when Mugabe took power I was in England; I did look for his name occasionally, but I don't know what became of him.

The question of relations between blacks and whites in what was then the Federation of Central Africa (Southern Rhodesia, Northern Rhodesia and Nyasaland) was buried, as usual, under a huge pile of sand and never discussed, except perhaps at dinner parties and then in a rather superficial way. But 'the natives were getting restless' and sometimes there were rather ugly protests and riots, very quickly put down with force. However, generally speaking, as in South Africa, the master–servant relationship continued to be the norm and on the surface everything was quiet. All this was to change in 1965 when some white politicians, led by Ian Smith, decided that the British government was about to upset their happy arrangement and, after what seemed like everlasting negotiations that always failed, declared independence. UDI arrived in our lives and with it sanctions imposed by the British government.

Once again I found myself living in a country with its white population divided as if by a knife. Those of us who opposed independence were a minority, about four thousand, and we clung together rather like a refugee group. We expressed our loyalty to the Crown and to the Governor of Rhodesia, Sir Humphrey Gibbs, in every way that we could, knowing all the time how utterly ineffectual it was. Smith meanwhile went from one madness to another. It really did smack of *Alice in Wonderland* when he was asked what were the benefits of independence and he replied, 'Well, independence.'

At the outset he announced that Rhodesia was an independent self-governing colony, loyal to the Queen ('no one is a more loyal subject of Her Majesty than I am') but when that didn't seem to work, Rhodesia, he decided, would become an independent republic with its own flag and its own national anthem and, of course, its own independent parliament. Wherever he went there were waving, cheering crowds of white people for whom he was the saviour who would protect them from the horrors of black domination. *For ever.* And the greater part of the white population believed him.

The tragedy was that instead of a gradual change in the status quo, with the black population slowly being included in government and finally becoming full partners in a black and white democracy, which was the dream of all those who opposed Ian Smith, his lunatic ideas were to lead inevitably to violence. Perhaps the vision of gradual change was never anything but a dream that would never have become reality, but it was the only hope for the country; to see it being destroyed was to lead to despair.

Sanctions-busting became a priority for the Rhodesian government and also for all the businesses operating in the country. Had it not been for the neighbouring countries, South Africa and Mozambique, Rhodesian independence would have come to an end much sooner than it did, but both these neighbouring countries co-operated with the Rhodesian government, shoring it up and enriching themselves at the same time. Rhodesia's principal requirement was fuel and the pipeline from Beira in Mozambique ensured a continual supply of petrol and at the same time thwarted the British government's sanctions policy. This turned most of us into hypocrites. We loathed the Smith regime and desperately wanted it to come to an end but we were jolly glad that we could go to a petrol station and put fuel into the tanks of our cars.

Geoffrey and I were to leave Rhodesia before the final onslaught of the 'Freedom War' with its toll of deaths of the black freedom fighters as they called themselves (the white population labelled them as terrorists). There were the equally tragic deaths of men in the white Rhodesian army. However, there was sporadic fighting and the outbreak of individual violent events even before we left. The Rhodesian government had by now brought into force conscription for all white males over the age of eighteen and there was absolutely no escape from this; inevitably when the war came there were deaths of some white soldiers who had no belief whatsoever in the cause for which they were compelled to fight. I think that the upper age limit for conscription was something like forty and Geoffrey was over that and so not involved.

While we continued to live in Rhodesia, our own personal lives were conducted in this strange, surreal atmosphere. David, Nickie and Bill were at school in Salisbury. David was one of the first five boys to attend St John's School when it opened. It is now a very large successful establishment with, I am told, some six hundred students. Our own family life was overshadowed by a great deal of sadness during these years as I was to suffer three miscarriages as well as the premature birth of a son who survived only for a very short while and whom I have mourned ever since. Then in 1962 there came the happiness of the safe arrival of Julian. Of course, we were both delighted by the birth of our son, but for Geoffrey to become a father for the first time at the age of forty-nine was completely overwhelming. Julian was to be his joy for the remaining years of his life.

About this time my mother married a very old family friend, Kenneth Grant Macleod, a man we all loved. He was a famous athlete, probably one of the finest all-round athletes ever produced in Scotland; he played rugby for Scotland while still a pupil at Fettes, was a double blue at Cambridge and twelfth man for the English cricket team. In sporting circles he was known as K. G. Macleod but to his family and friends he was Grant. He owned race horses, which my mother loved, and they had a short but very happy life together. Sadly, Grant developed cancer and died after only three years of their marriage. We mourned him and I felt that I had lost a loving and supportive stepfather.

I had imagined, foolishly, that after our marriage we would live in England but, Geoffrey had a job in Salisbury and resolutely refused to consider any of the ideas I had for leaving. It grieves me now to think how much he must have hated it and how deeply he must have felt trapped by his financial responsibilities for the whole of the eighteen years we were there. I did try so hard to get away from Africa but I failed until 1971.

Wanting to leave was nothing new. I had always wondered how I could escape. Even when I was at school I felt that there must be better things and better places elsewhere; places where there were beautiful things to see and hear and where there was more of interest and excitement. It was a dream to change what seemed like fate and get away to the other side of the world, but I had to wait for a very long time before the dream came true. Of course, even now, after living in England for longer than I lived in Africa, there are flashes, memories of trivial things, that bring it all back. It was, after all, home. Sometimes the memories are good, especially when I hear, perhaps on the radio, the sound of African voices singing in harmony or remember the smell of the leaves of plants growing alongside the beach at St James in the Cape, or visualise a dry, dusty path in Rhodesia, I feel a certain nostalgia – but not for long.

In January 1972 Geoffrey was due to retire from the Shell company for which he worked and, as we thought that Julian should start school at the beginning of the school year, Julian and I left for England in August 1971. Of course, there had been much discussion about where he should go and Geoffrey had travelled to England early in 1971 to look at schools. With hindsight I think we made a huge mistake and that we should have settled on a place to live and sent Julian to a day school, but we thought we were doing the best for him and that he would enjoy boarding school. Life at home as an only child, we thought, with the others now all grown up, would not be good for him. Geoffrey was very impressed by the Junior School of Cheltenham College and Julian was entered there.

It was decided that Julian and I would have a base in London while I looked for a house to buy and we rented a flat in Beaufort Gardens. The flat was in a house owned by two very charming spinster sisters, the Misses Milnes, and completely furnished, consisting of two bedrooms, a very good living room plus a cleaner for four hours a week. All this cost £20 per week. Before he went to school and in the holidays, Julian and I were very happy in Beaufort Gardens. It is incredible to imagine now but, aged nine, he would walk alone to Harrods and spend the entire morning in the toy department, where the very kind and civilised employees allowed him to play with any of the toys. He got to know Harrods like the back of his hand. My job was to find a house but unfortunately this was at the height of the gazumping season. There were no houses for sale, it seemed, and as soon as one heard of one and before one could get there, the price had gone up or it was sold. Geoffrey did not want to live in London and so I was looking within a fairly small radius of Cheltenham. Of course, I actually knew very little about living in England and had not much idea about what to look for. It was not an easy task.

I dashed about the country, taking the train to somewhere and then hiring a car to go and view a house. Something went wrong every time until I was told about Thorn House in Steeple Ashton in Wiltshire and, with fear of gazumping driving the need for speedy decisions, I bought it. This was in December 1971 and Geoffrey, who was to arrive at the end of January 1972, had said that he did not want to be in London when he arrived and so, very sadly, we moved out of Beaufort Gardens and into a

cemetery. Geoffrey returned home immediately. David and Bill, who were in London, came down to Steeple Ashton, and Julian, now eleven, was told of her death on the following Sunday when he was at home.

Death makes one feel that all life should stop altogether, but it doesn't, and gradually, very slowly, what seems unendurable becomes endurable. We went on with our lives in Steeple Ashton and John and the children returned to a house outside Oxford. Thorn House was finally finished and we both loved it and loved the garden and liked the village.

My proud boast is that the woman who ran the WI met two gay men with whom we had become friendly who lived in the village and asked, 'Do you know Moira Bennett?' 'Yes,' came the answer. 'We like her very much.' 'Oh, I'm sure she's very nice, but not WI material.' I want NOT WI MATERIAL engraved on my tombstone.

Despite my deficiencies, we made a few friends, Geoffrey had a part-time job in the bursar's office at Cheltenham Ladies College and was elected the Conservative member of the District Council, work he enjoyed. On the surface all seemed well. However, he was not looking at all well and was suffering with very bad back pain.

ALDEBURGH

We took Julian for a short, very enjoyable break in Paris but every year when the question of a holiday had come up, the decision was always to go to Aldeburgh on the Suffolk coast where Geoffrey and Julian loved sailing and where we had sailing friends. I longed for Italy or Spain or something a bit more exotic than East Anglia but I was in the minority and Aldeburgh it always was. I began to think that, despite loving our house, if we moved and went to live in Aldeburgh, perhaps we would be able to go to one of these more exciting places when we went on holiday. More seriously, the children in Wiltshire were interested only in the Pony Club, which Julian most definitely wasn't, but he did adore sailing. I thought that he would have a much happier life in Aldeburgh and I knew that Geoffrey would love it and feel at home. All his childhood holidays had been spent in Walberswick where his parents had a holiday house and Suffolk was very familiar ground for him. And so in the summer of 1975, in Aldeburgh, I suggested this to Geoffrey and he replied that he would be happy with that but it was my job to find a house.

It didn't take me long. There were never many houses for sale in the best part of Aldeburgh, up on top of the terrace and near the centre of the town, but we were very lucky that Maureen Ramsden-Knowles, an acquaintance, agreed to sell us her house in Beaconsfield Road. This was in August and in December 1975 we moved. Although I was very keen to be in Aldeburgh and I was convinced it was the right thing to do, I was terribly worried about Geoffrey's health. He was looking very unwell and although, typically, he never complained, I began to be very anxious.

In January 1976 he was quite suddenly and obviously very ill and we began the long journey of medical investigation and tests, all of which were to prove negative. Finally, in March, it was decided that he should undergo an exploratory operation with the result that terminal cancer of the liver was diagnosed. The surgeon rather brutally told him that he only had six months to live and ordered a course of steroids, saying to me, 'He will feel better and he will look better, but don't be fooled.'

With these words, we started out on Geoffrey's last six months. We told Julian that his father was very ill, which he could see for himself, but we didn't tell him the true situation, and he continued in the rhythm of boarding school life at Cheltenham College. It was the summer of 1976, the long, hot dry summer when every day the sun shone, the grass turned brown and the sky was cloudless. Geoffrey did, indeed, start to feel better and there was much that he enjoyed in those wonderful, hot summer days. We went sailing with Henry and Pat Joscelyn, old friends of his who lived near Ipswich, and the days on the water gave him real pleasure. He enjoyed Aldeburgh and enjoyed living by the sea and somehow, agonisingly, the months passed.

On 6 November Geoffrey died. (In view of the direction my life was about to take, it is extraordinary that Benjamin Britten should have died almost exactly one month later.) It was only three years since Nickie's death and I went through bereavement again. Poor Julian suffered the loss of his adored father. Bill was around but David was now living in Australia and, of course, Nickie was gone. Julian and I were very much on our own. Geoffrey had a sister in Southwold but she offered little support and I suppose had her own problems, so we hardly ever saw her. We felt very bereft of the support of a family but we were lucky in our friends.

It was not long before I realised that more money was going out than was coming in and decided that I must find a way to earn something. I wanted to be at home when Julian was back from school so, in a moment of madness, I decided to become a picture framer, working from home. I went on a course to learn how to do it and then set up my stall. Work started to come in but I began to hate it. Firstly, because it was a very lonely occupation and secondly because I was using extremely sharp knives and I became terrified that I would cut myself and bleed all over one of the valuable pictures that had been brought to me. It was not a success.

Next I became a 'Universal Aunt' employed by families to look after the house and children while the parents went on holiday. My first experience was in Kingston and I marvelled at the trust that was placed in me. As I arrived at the address the mother more or less said, 'Here are the keys of the house, here are the keys of the car, please feed the cat', and waltzed out to drive to Heathrow. There were two teenage daughters, plus a ten-year-old boy, and she said that the teenagers might upset me as they quarrelled, non-stop, very noisily. On the first night after I'd given them supper the two girls started to yell at each other but I didn't really care and went on reading my book. That was the end of it. They never quarrelled again while I was there and turned out to be very nice girls.

After a spell in Connaught Square with dreadfully spoilt American children, I went to an ultra-Orthodox Jewish family in North London where there was one twelve-year-old girl. This was the best job I had and I got to like her very much. Next was a family in Hampstead Garden Suburb where there was a little boy of about eight who was supposed to be at school every day but was violently ill the first night I was there, and could not go to school for the whole period. This made me decide to find something else to do; I hadn't much liked cleaning up sick for my own children and I certainly didn't want to do it for others.

I had been in touch for some time with Father Martin Israel, a remarkable Anglican priest who was also a pathologist at one of the main London teaching hospitals, and he was very anxious for me to become a psychotherapist. This was in the days before there were more therapists than patients. I was very interested in his plan, despite the fact that it would have entailed a three-year course in London but, quite unexpectedly, a friend in Aldeburgh suggested that I should try to get a job with the Aldeburgh Festival and, being very ignorant, I thought that it might be a good idea. If I had known more about the brilliant and distinguished people I would be working for and the clever young people with whom I would work, I would never have dared to ask for a job.

At exactly this time there was a major outbreak of salmonella in Aldeburgh and I was one of those most severely affected. I said afterwards to the doctor, 'I really thought I might die', and he replied, 'Don't worry, Moira, I thought so too.' I had had lunch at the Festival Club and, foolishly, ate the chicken mayonnaise, which tasted delicious but was actually crawling with salmonella. Altogether seventy-two people were ill; five of them, including me, very seriously ill. The Club was owned and run by the Aldeburgh Festival and Bill Servaes, the General Manager, was afraid that he would face litigation and endless claims. So, when I rang up and asked to see him, he was sure that that was the reason for my visit.

'No, no,' I explained. 'I've come to ask you for a job.' He was amazed but said, 'Well, we are just about to open the new building of the Britten–Pears School; we are employing two young men and I think that if we had a third and rather older member of staff, it would be a good thing. The hours are anti-social and the salary is derisory but would you like to start on a three-month trial basis?' Absolutely, I would, and at the age of fifty-four my career in arts administration began.

IT WAS NOT JUST A CAREER in arts administration that had started. My entire life was to change completely, so much so that I feel that it has been divided into two – all that went before and all that came after my job at Aldeburgh. And not only did my life change but I changed too. Until then I had lived a life in Africa with all the limitations that that entailed and then a domestic life in England, gradually becoming more controlled by habit, my thinking formed by the circumstances of a very conventional life. Suddenly everything was changed and I felt as though a grenade had exploded in my head, transforming me utterly. Of course this is not quite true. We are the result of our genetic make-up and all that we have experienced during our lives; change is built on what has gone before. However, I did feel at the time, and still feel, that somehow I became a different person.

ALDEBURGH

WHEN I ACCEPTED Bill Servaes's offer, I really had no idea that my entire life would undergo a complete transformation and that what it would be in the future would bear very little relation to what it had been up until that point. I thought that I was just accepting a job; I did not realise that what I was accepting would place me in a new world, a world of which I knew nothing and that just about everything about me, including my way of thinking, would have to change. Aged fifty-four, I had led such a conventional and constrained life, a life in which I had hardly even heard of Benjamin Britten and Peter Pears. Suddenly all that was gone and I found myself forced to adapt to this new world as quickly as possible. It was certainly not just a career in arts administration that had started.

I believe that this could have happened only at Aldeburgh. For one thing, no other arts organisation, and certainly no prestigious arts organisation in any of the cities of the world, would have even considered employing me, a woman in her fifties with no experience. Nor do I believe that elsewhere I would have been promoted to the job that I held later and where I held such responsibility and from which I derived such enjoyment. It could not have happened anywhere else but Aldeburgh. The atmosphere there at the time is quite hard to describe: it had an informal, rural, almost amateurish side to it, with local people employed in various roles, people who previously had absolutely no experience of the arts. On the other hand, some of the brightest young stars of the world of arts administration were working in the organisation, led by a luminary of Peter Pears's distinction. I suppose that part of the informality might have been due to the way in which the whole Aldeburgh enterprise began, when Britten and Pears knew all the working people in Aldeburgh and gathered them in to help, when some of Britten's greatest operas were performed in the Jubilee Hall, which was the equivalent of a village hall. There was always this curious mixture of an international concert hall on one side and the village hall on the other, and the atmosphere this mixture produced pervaded the whole organisation and everything that we did.

However, before I begin to tell the story of my career in Aldeburgh, I think that, for the benefit of anyone who is unfamiliar with the Aldeburgh Festival, the Britten–Pears School for Advanced Musical Studies and all the other activities that have developed since the start of the Festival, I should produce a sort of instruction manual, a very short guide to tell a little of the history, describe the landscape and explain the structure of the whole organisation. Otherwise I am sure that what I write will be completely mystifying.

Aldeburgh is a very old town on the east coast of England, battered by sea and wind, and for centuries a centre for boat building, fishing and smuggling. Due to changes to the river Alde, the boat-building industry moved elsewhere, most of the smuggling stopped and only the fishermen remained and now, in the twenty-first century, even the fishermen hardly exist. Gradually the town, too, changed and became a great place for second homes and for holiday-makers, who in summer fill all the B & Bs, the hotels and the caravan park outside Aldeburgh. The old shops in the High Street have gone and in their place are boutiques and restaurants; only the bookshop and the fish and chip shop are the same as they have always been. In summer it is not only holiday-makers who throng in Aldeburgh High Street but international musicians, concertgoers and students who are drawn to all the musical activities that started with the Aldeburgh Festival. Although this has brought unparalleled prosperity to the town, its original old families, now rather few and far between, still view the newcomers with deep suspicion. They are always outsiders. Britten himself seems to have been exempt from this suspicion: he was, after all, a local lad, born in Lowestoft; he knew all the Aldeburgh people and had an easy and warm relationship with the fishermen and the people who lived there. The continuity with the past that they represented was important for him and they were his friends.

After some time in the United States but still before the end of the Second World War, Benjamin Britten and Peter Pears came to live in Suffolk, first in the village of Snape a few miles inland, where Britten had had a home since 1937, and then in Aldeburgh itself. In 1948 they started the Aldeburgh Festival. It was small at the beginning but it is now one of the most important and distinguished arts festivals in the world, a magnet for international music-lovers. At the start all the Festival events took place in Aldeburgh, in the Parish Church, the Jubilee Hall and the Baptist Chapel in the High Street. It soon became apparent that a much larger home – in fact a concert hall that could double as an opera house – was needed and in 1965 negotiations were begun to lease the redundant maltings, where formerly barley was prepared for brewing, at Snape.

Snape was at one time more important than Aldeburgh. The remains of Saxon burial grounds, including ship and boat burials, are found nearby and later there was a well-known racetrack where very popular race meetings were held. Over time Snape lost its importance; the village had been ravaged during the plague, which killed a large number of its inhabitants, and all the work went elsewhere. However, in the nineteenth century, Snape Maltings was established and became a successful business employing most of the men who lived in the village. Its demise due to market changes in 1965, when the owners, Swonnells & Sons of Lowestoft, were obliged to sell all the buildings, brought great hardship and serious unemployment to Snape. George Gooderham, a Suffolk farmer, bought the whole site, including the actual maltings itself, with its iconic roof, and all the ancillary buildings. It was the maltings that was to become the Snape Maltings Concert Hall.

The lease of the maltings was successfully negotiated with George Gooderham by Britten and his colleagues and the architectural and engineering firm Arup was commissioned to convert it into a concert hall. The only other buildings included in the lease were those that actually adjoined the concert hall and it was one of these, originally the granary, that later became the Britten–Pears School for Advanced Musical Studies. As the Festival developed, Britten and Pears saw the need for post-conservatory performance studies and they started to dream of an education centre. They began with very informal masterclasses, often in their own home. Britten's death in 1976 gave fresh impetus to the scheme as it was decided that it should serve as a permanent memorial to him and in 1979 the old granary building was converted into the School.

The concert hall and the School were included in the lease but Gooderham remained the owner of the site and all the other buildings. Over the years he allowed these to fall into disrepair and it all looked very run down; the

Aldeburgh Foundation was frequently criticised for allowing all the paint to peel off the outbuildings by concertgoers who did not realise that the upkeep of the rest of the site was not the Foundation's responsibility.

Administrative structures needed to be put in place as the activities grew and developed, with a parent body established for both the School and the Festival: in those days it was called the Aldeburgh Festival–Snape Maltings Foundation, a cumbersome title that was later shortened to the Aldeburgh Foundation. There was a Board of Trustees for the Aldeburgh Foundation and an Education Committee formed specifically to oversee the activities of the School but the day-to-day running of both was the responsibility of the general manager of the Aldeburgh Foundation.

I have written the history of the Britten–Pears School in a book, *Making Musicians*, which was published in May 2012. Although there is, inevitably, a certain amount in the book that is personal, my task was to write an objective history of the School. Now I am writing my own story, following my career in arts administration, beginning with the Britten–Pears School for Advanced Musical Studies.

KEEPING THE COURSES RUNNING

Summer courses had not yet begun when I joined the staff of the School and a less qualified person than me could hardly be imagined. I was older by a very long way than the other two members of staff, fifty-four to their twenty-two. Although I had always listened to music and, like every other girl of my generation, learned the piano at school, my experience was limited to that and my actual knowledge of music could have been written on the back of a postage stamp. I was to work with two bright young men, John Owen and John Evans, and it is to their credit that they welcomed me warmly, were polite and helpful, although I think they must have been rather horrified and had serious doubts about what actual use I could be to the team. Obviously, I had to learn absolutely everything from scratch and when I realised just how much this would be, I was terrified and appalled by my ignorance.

The two young men were both busy organising the courses which were shortly to start (John Evans had responsibility for the vocal courses and John Owen for the string courses) and I was supposed to help with the secretarial work and the accommodation for students. It was, in a way, my first 'proper' job, as what I had done during the war was rather different. I must have tried the patience of my colleagues to breaking point. I look back now and wonder how I had the cheek to think that I could do it and certainly if I had had any real understanding of my inadequacies, I would never have dared go to Bill Servaes to ask for a job, let alone accept one.

But there I was and I just had to make the best of it. We would all decamp to the brand new School building in Snape once the courses began but at the very beginning the three of us were in one room in the Aldeburgh Festival offices in the former Suffolk Hotel in Aldeburgh High Street. About three weeks after I started, we were ready to move our offices to the School and to prepare for the arrival of the students. After the scruffiness of the Suffolk Hotel, the beauty of the new School building at Snape, so recently opened, was breathtaking. Converted, like the concert hall, by Arup, it was very simple with the bare brick retained, very plain, decorated and finished in pale neutral colours and overlooking the Suffolk marshes with their ever-changing light; it was truly a magical place. I think we all felt a certain degree of awe that we were to work in this marvellous building and that we were the first people to do so. I remember how scared we were of marking the pale carpet on the stairs.

The students were post-graduate young musicians, selected by a rigorous audition process from a pool of outstanding talent, who came to Snape to take part in masterclasses, directed by some of the most distinguished musicians in the world. When the courses began and they all arrived, I felt as though I had suddenly been engulfed in a raging storm, a hurricane, from which I would not emerge, battered and only just standing, ten weeks later when the 1979 courses ended. I suppose the boys felt differently and had an understanding of the shape of the whole season, but I certainly did not and I remained terrified; I am told now that I hid my fear very well but, at the time, it was horribly real for me. The pattern of courses was to change later, but in those early days the courses each ran for an entire week, back to back for the whole period, with the working day often not ending before 10 p.m. The staff was free only on Sunday mornings. I had no time to think about anything except what I had to do the very next minute.

At 2 p.m. on Sundays the new students would arrive to go through a registration process and to be given details of their accommodation, the schedules and general information. The students all looked like students, rather scruffy, and for some time I found it difficult to distinguish one from another. We all went into the wonderful, newly designed, Recital Room for a sing-through (or play-through) with the course directors, repetiteurs and coaches. At around 6 p.m. we finished and the students went back into Aldeburgh for an evening meal.

For the rest of the week the School day began at 9 a.m. when the School bus would drive the students out from Aldeburgh, where they were accommodated, to start the School day, which was filled with masterclasses, practice, and consultations; officially it ended at 6 p.m., everyone having had a short break for coffee in the morning and a light lunch. However on many evenings there was an additional lecture or some activity linked to the course and we often closed the School at 10 p.m. and limped back to home in Aldeburgh and bed. This was the pattern from Monday to Friday. On Saturday there was a rehearsal followed by a concert in the concert hall in the evening ending at about 10 p.m. At 2 p.m. on Sunday the whole thing started again with new students.

In *Making Musicians*, I have described my work at this time, a large part of which was spent trying to get the students fed; in pre-microwave days the facilities in our canteen were limited and really consisted of an electric kettle and not much else. There was tea and coffee and sandwiches. As the catering was so limited, it was my job to go to the Aldeburgh bakery every day and bring out the fresh buns and the fillings of cheese and ham. Their evening meals were the students' own responsibility. They had all been given a huge 'full English' breakfast by the wonderful Aldeburgh landladies with whom they lived, and we knew that, despite the dull sandwich lunches, which were the best we could do, they were very well fed. Another of my tasks was to arrange the transport from Aldeburgh to Snape for classes and liaise with the Aldeburgh Festival accommodation officer to ensure that all the students were in the right place with the right landlady and happy to be there. It was truly dogsbody work but it demanded all my concentration.

As well as trying to remember what I had to do, I also had to learn the culture of the place, which was entirely foreign to me. The greater part of that culture was based around Britten and Pears. The stature of Britten, who had died only three years earlier, was immense and was present all the time; there was constant talk of Ben, what Ben would have liked, what

top The Britten–Pears School and the Snape Maltings Concert Hall in 1979
bottom left The Concert Hall across the fields at Snape
bottom right The porch of the Britten–Pears School under construction

top left Assistants at the School: myself, John Evans and John Owen
top right The entrance to our offices in Aldeburgh High Street
bottom left Mstislav Rostropovich with John Owen and John Evans,
backstage at the Maltings Concert Hall in 1979
bottom right Hugh Maguire, the School's first Director of String Studies,
with John Owen, in 1980

Sir Peter Pears, the Founder and Director of Singing Studies, teaching
at the Britten–Pears School in 1979 (*top*) and 1982 (*below*)

Teachers at the Britten–Pears School:
Artur Balsam (*top left*, 1978), Murray Perahia (*top right*, 1979)
William Pleeth (*bottom left*, 1977) and Jacqueline du Pré (*bottom right*, 1979)

Ben would have done, so much so that it was almost as though he was a living presence dominating our lives. Peter Pears was very much a live presence, involved with the School on a daily basis, teaching during the singers' courses and taking an interest in everything that happened. From those first days until his death in 1986 he was always kind to me and I came to place great value on his friendship.

We had the most distinguished musicians teaching and at the start I was very much in awe of them. I remember seeing Murray Perahia standing in the queue with the students, waiting for a cup of coffee, and thinking that it was wrong and that someone ought to get his coffee for him. However, before long I realised that everybody, including the stars, were there to do their work and it gradually became a job of which we were all a part.

As well as Peter Pears, the other regular members of the teaching staff who were at the School all the time during courses were Nancy Evans and Hugh Maguire. Nancy Evans, who was to become Co-Director of Singing Studies, had been a star and had had a very successful career; she had frequently performed with Peter Pears, with whom she had a close friendship. She was a very pretty woman, sweet and gentle, with an unexpectedly sharp wit and a wonderful sense of humour. We all loved her. Hugh Maguire was the director of string studies while still leading the Orchestra of the Royal Opera House. A great violinist, he had in his youth been considered a wunderkind and he had performed with all the most highly regarded musicians. I remember seeing a video that had been made from a rather grainy old film of Hugh in rehearsal with his great friends, Daniel Barenboim and Jacqueline du Pré and finding their youth, their laughter and high spirits very moving. Hugh was now older and grey haired but the Irish charm was still very much a part of him. He was uncompromising as a director of string studies and demanded the very highest standards from everyone; his sternness if he suspected that these standards were not being upheld might have come as a surprise to some students.

I am sure that everyone involved understood what was happening and had in their minds an overall picture of all the courses – who was coming to teach, what each course would cover and where the students had come from – but for a long time I felt as though I was in a foreign country where I did not understand a word of the language. After about five or six weeks I decided that I simply could not go on. I was very tired; I felt that the physical demands were too high, and the unwelcome truth was that I was just not up to it.

I went to bed, exhausted as usual, having made up my mind that I would have to go to see Bill Servaes, thank him for giving me the opportunity and tell him that I simply could not do it. I fell asleep happier that I had made this decision but during the night I woke up and started thinking about it all. How absolutely pathetic, I thought. What a wimp I was being. I thought about this for some time before I fell asleep again, knowing that I could not allow myself to be defeated so easily and that the next day and every day after that I would just get up, go to work and do the best that I could. The curious thing about all this was that, although I was often very tired, I was never utterly exhausted again and the whole idea of giving up became unimaginable. That taught me a lesson.

The first course in that first year in the School building was a chamber music course for wind, strings and piano, directed by Artur Balsam, Thea King, Murray Perahia and Wolfgang Melhorn. Artur Balsam, a highly respected pianist himself, had been one of Perahia's teachers in New York and it was he who had persuaded Balsam to come to Snape to teach – a considerable coup for the School. (Mieczysław Horszowski, the great pianist who was still performing when he was over ninety, had been Perahia's principal teacher.) Aged seventy-three when he came to Snape, Artur Balsam was a very tiny man and very dapper; he always wore a three-piece suit and had eyes that positively glittered with humour.

He was accompanied by Mrs Balsam, a rather large and forbidding woman, and when they first arrived I was told that I had to go and meet them at the Wentworth Hotel as they were not happy with the room they had been given. I found them in the foyer of the hotel and they explained they had been given a room with a double bed, which was quite impossible for them. I spoke to Mike Pritt, whose father owned the Wentworth, and after a time, during which I sat and chatted to the Balsams, we were taken down a long corridor to inspect a room with single beds. Mike Pritt and Mrs Balsam walked ahead and to my astonishment Artur Balsam, who was very much shorter than me, suddenly flung his arms around my waist and said in his accented English, 'I find you instantly adorable.' Instantly adorable or not and very aware of Mrs Balsam's back a few yards in front of us, I tried to put the tiny man down, saying very quietly, 'Mr Balsam, stop it.' No word was ever said again but from the expression in those humorous eyes of his, I knew that there could be a repeat at any moment. Despite this unusual start, I liked him very much. He was clever and interesting and I enjoyed listening to him and Murray talking about music and reminiscing about the days when Perahia had been his pupil. From the way he talked it was obvious that from the first he recognised Murray Perahia's extraordinary talent and knew that he would reach the highest peaks in his musical career. It was obvious, too, that he was fond of Murray and that he would be forgiven, when talking of his youthful pupil, for saying jokingly, 'My God, was he sentimental – I had to stop that.'

Courses proceeded through the summer. There were string courses with the enormously admired cello teacher William Pleeth and academic courses, one on Vaughan Williams with Ursula, his widow, progressing around the School like the prow of a mighty ship. There was an unforgettable day when Jacqueline du Pré, accompanied by a nurse and already desperately ill, came to Snape with Daniel Barenboim, her husband, to give a masterclass. I shall never forget her courage.

With every day I learned a little more and I was grateful that there appeared to be no disasters. Gradually that year's courses came to an end, leaving John Owen with a truly dreadful cough, John Evans thin and white with exhaustion and me stumbling about with tiredness. We were all thankful that now we would have some time off but, at the same time, there was a general sense of achievement, a feeling that it had been a good year and that a lot had been achieved. During that first year and all the other years, we were working closely with the staff of the Aldeburgh Festival. Hilary Keenlyside, a very popular colleague, had been working for the School before the building opened and was now appointed the Festival concerts manager; her predecessor was Jenni Vaulkhard (now Wake-Walker) who had been close to both Britten and Pears and had made a great success of the job.

There were to be several changes in 1980 and the School staff changed. John Evans left to take up a research appointment at the Britten–Pears Library and Jessica Ford took his place. It was decided that we needed secretarial help and an American, Virginia Caldwell, became a well-liked and valued member of the team. During 1979 the three of us had got by and had tolerated each another's foibles and differences and, in my case, the lamentable lack of relevant experience. All this was to change in

1980 and I look back on it as one of the worst and unhappiest of all the years I was to spend in arts administration. Suddenly and unexpectedly there was dislike, mistrust and suspicion and the atmosphere changed radically. Our two regular and popular Canadian repetiteurs, Stephen Ralls and Bruce Ubukata, were certainly aware of what was happening and I am sure that Hugh Maguire knew too, but generally speaking it was well concealed and none of the students or the rest of the teaching staff had any idea of our difficulties. Were it not for the fact that I felt so strongly that I must not give up, I am not sure that I would have lasted much longer.

I found myself with another quite unconnected problem. After Geoffrey's death in 1976, I made a lot of friends in Aldeburgh, some of them really just acquaintances but to some, who had been very kind and understanding, I had become close. When Bill Servaes originally offered me a job I knew that it really was an all-or-nothing choice and that if I accepted his offer, there would be no time for anything else; my life would become my work. I imagined that friends would understand this. And mostly they did but, to my surprise, I found it was not always the case and I encountered quite unexpected jealousy. There I was working my guts out and I certainly did not think that anyone would find it enviable or become jealous, but I suppose that most people's lives in Aldeburgh were rather limited; so many were retired and there was golf, bridge or sailing and that was that. Perhaps it was obvious that I was having fun and doing something interesting but I found the tension with former friends quite upsetting and an unwanted distraction. From the beginning it had been a matter of choice and I had chosen, knowing that social life would have to take second place. In spite of these difficulties, it was the best choice I ever made.

Courses in 1980 followed much the same pattern as 1979. As part of the programme the School produced two performances of Britten's *Albert Herring* in Snape Maltings Concert Hall directed by Eric Crozier, the librettist and Nancy Evans's husband. It was for me tremendously exciting and I loved having a part, however small, in the work behind the production. It was also the year that we had the Tel Aviv Quartet directing the string quartet course and the Beaux Arts Trio teaching the piano trio course. It was heady stuff for someone with my background.

Donald Mitchell, the director of academic courses, who had become fascinated by the music of Thailand, brought the Royal Court Thai musicians to Snape in 1980 for a series of courses. When the Thai musicians performed on their strange instruments and dressed in what looked like fancy dress, we had to remove several rows of seats in our Recital Room as they were very disturbed by feet and couldn't bear to be near them. That was something new for me to learn.

The year ended sadly when on 1 December Peter Pears suffered a stroke, which left him with a paralysed arm and very restricted movement in one leg and made walking difficult. He was tremendously brave and undertook regular exercises and physiotherapy, which gradually made walking easier. The School had always been a passionate interest of his but now teaching and the School took foremost place in his life.

The year 1981 brought further changes to the School and to its parent body. Jessica Ford left; Virginia Caldwell continued to work as the School secretary, and John Owen was appointed course administrator with overall responsibility for both the singers' and string players' courses. I, who had been labelled the administrative assistant, was now called the registrar, but in reality, although I now worked much more closely with John Owen and was given further responsibilities, my role did not change very much. My admiration for John Owen at this time and in all his subsequent years at the School is boundless. In *Making Musicians* I wrote a great deal about the contribution he made to the School and it would certainly not have flourished as it did without his unfailing commitment. I must say that from a personal point of view I learned an enormous amount from him but it was not only a case of being guided by him; it was in 1981 that our friendship really took root and continues unchanged to this day.

In 1981 when we were working in Aldeburgh and not at the actual School, I was given a different office, a rather small office where I was alone. I complained that every morning when I came in, there was a dreadful smell of gas. An engineer was sent for and he inspected the pipes in a fairly desultory sort of way, I thought, and then pronounced that there was no leak and that all was well. So every day I sat there in a room that smelled of gas. Some years later, when the Aldeburgh Foundation moved out of the old Suffolk Hotel, I was told that there was utter horror when it was discovered that under the floorboards in what had been my office, gas was leaking absolutely unhindered and had been leaking for years. I had been very lucky and, after the salmonella episode, I suppose the Foundation was too – not because I wasn't dead but because there was no litigation.

The changes that 1981 brought affected us very much and completely changed for the better the dynamics of the relationships among the School staff, but the greater change took place at the Aldeburgh Foundation. The general manager, Bill Servaes, to whom I owed such a debt of gratitude and who had trusted me enough to offer me the job in the first place, resigned and Jack Phipps was appointed in his place. As Bill Servaes said to someone at the time, 'There is not a square inch of my back that is not a knife wound.' This might be the moment to address what I called 'the Aldeburgh disease'.

THE ALDEBURGH CULTURE

Although Britten was adored and had great charisma it is obvious that he was a person who was very quick to take offence and that offence was not quickly forgiven. There is no better demonstration of this than the way in which Stephen Reiss, an early general manager, was obliged to resign, having suddenly fallen out of favour. Reiss had been a crucial figure in the early days of the Aldeburgh Festival; he had originally identified the maltings as a possible building for conversion into a concert hall and he had played a vital role in the rebuilding programme following the devastating fire that took place in 1969. His obituary in the *Guardian* described him as 'one of a long line of talented people who helped develop the Aldeburgh Festival and then found themselves out in the cold'.

There are endless tales of artists who were close to Britten and Pears and who were expelled and not reinstated for years, if ever. Eric Crozier was one of these, as was Basil Coleman, the opera and television director, and there were many others. John Amis told me that having been a welcome member of the inner circle he, inexplicably, found himself out in the cold, only to be welcomed back to the warmth some years later. 'I never knew the reason for my expulsion or for my return.' It is not hard to imagine the atmosphere of mistrust and suspicion that flourished.

When I joined the staff Britten had been dead for three years and yet this atmosphere still prevailed. I was astonished to discover all the factions and the way they seemed to dislike one another. There was the 'office', meaning the Foundation administration, led by Bill Servaes;

there were Donald Mitchell and Isador Caplan representing the Trustees of the Britten–Pears Foundation, very powerful figures, a duo who had always been close to Britten and who were known by Bill Servaes as 'the ayatollahs'; and then there was the Red House and the Britten–Pears Library. The Red House which was the home of Britten and Pears was now lived in by Peter alone. He was a much milder person, but he had his own staff and they and the Library staff formed another little clique. Fortunately there was at Red House the benign influence of Rita Thomson, the wonderful Scottish woman who had been Britten's nurse. She stayed on after his death as Peter Pears's companion, beloved and admired by all who knew her. Her loyalty was absolute and she managed to remain above all the machinations that took place around her.

I saw for myself the distrust and scheming early on in my days at Aldeburgh. There had been an enquiry into the structure and management of the Foundation, conducted over a fairly long period by one of the then fashionable consultants who were beginning to spring into life everywhere. We had all been interviewed and a confidential report was to be produced. A member of the Foundation staff, well known to me, discovered that the report had arrived, that it was at the Red House and that Pears's secretary had seen it. The staff member, who held a senior position, rushed up to the secretary with whom she was friendly and persuaded her to reveal what was in the report. With breath-taking duplicity, she then told Pears that his secretary had shown her the report, which resulted in the secretary's instant dismissal. How's that for backstabbing!

There was dislike and perhaps jealousy, too, among some of the artistic directors and they schemed and plotted against one another. The atmosphere all round was far from sunny. Apart from the year 1980 when I myself had been the victim of distrust and dishonesty, I was mercifully unaffected by all this and everybody was kind and supportive to me. Later, when Kenneth Baird became the general manager, he did much to shed light into dark corners and the atmosphere became a great deal better. It was under his management that I spent the majority of my years at Aldeburgh and so I was fortunate; we were all aware of the suspicion around us and what I call the 'disease' persisted for many years, with distrust between the staff at the Red House and the Library towards the management of the Festival and the School. Two recent appointments, of Roger Wright as chief executive of

Snape Maltings (formerly Aldeburgh Music) and Sarah Bardwell as general director of the Britten–Pears Foundation, are doing much to bring an end to the dark atmosphere that has bedevilled Aldeburgh for so long.

In 1981 the change when Jack Phipps was appointed general manager after Bill Servaes could not have been greater. Bill was a stickler for correct, impeccable behaviour; he always maintained the highest standards in dress and manner and did his best to ensure that his staff did the same. He loathed anything that smacked of slackness or a slapdash attitude and we all took our cue from him and learned a lot that I am sure has stood us all in good stead. Jack Phipps, by contrast, was very informal. I remember my astonishment when I first saw him tieless after a concert in the Maltings. (It must be remembered that in those days men always wore a tie for formal occasions.) He was married to Sue, Peter Pears's niece, and this by itself inevitably made everyone view the appointment with a degree of suspicion. Jack came from the Arts Council and he wanted to stage huge, ambitious projects and did not seem to understand that we did not have the Arts Council's budget. That the whole operation was run on a shoestring seemed to have escaped him. He proceeded to spend the little money that we did have like the proverbial drunken sailor.

However, it is thanks to Jack that my career, and indeed my life, was to change again and change quite dramatically. One day, unexpectedly, he said that he wanted to see me and we had a conversation in the School office. 'I want to launch a new, large capital appeal and I also want to open a sponsorship department. I think you are the right person to head both the appeal and sponsorship. Please think about it and let me have your answer.' I was never more surprised and I went home with my head buzzing. Soon afterwards I spoke to Alan Russell. Alan had been a distinguished figure in the City, was now retired and living in Aldeburgh. He and his wife, Jean, were the very best friends that anyone could ever want, always loyal, supportive and kind. His wisdom and experience made him the obvious person to go to for advice, but what he said was unexpected: 'Don't touch it. Sponsorship and fundraising for a capital sum is now highly professional and you have no idea how to do it. You've got a nice job at the School and you should just carry on doing it.'

I felt rather deflated and I went home to consider what Alan had said and what I felt myself. It seemed to me that all fundraising was really a matter of common sense and I couldn't see why I could not do it. So ignoring the advice, I went to Jack and said yes. He was pleased but I was horrified when I asked who would take my place at the School and he answered, 'Well, I think that my Sue would be the right person to be the Head of the School.' With that remark I understood the motive behind the offer and felt that, although the outcome might work well for me, I had nevertheless walked into a trap. My knowledge of how the School staff operated and the personalities involved made me believe that Sue was certainly not the person to take my job and that, besides, the whole thing would smack of nepotism. I could hardly say that and so I probably just murmured something meaningless.

The chairman of the Aldeburgh Foundation had until shortly before this been Lord Inverforth but he had tragically collapsed and died on his fiftieth birthday as the result of an asthma attack, five days before the start of the thirty-fifth Aldeburgh Festival. Peter Du Sautoy, formerly the chairman of the publishing house Faber and Faber, and now living in Aldeburgh with his wife Mollie, both great friends of Britten, had taken an active role in the work of the Foundation and was now the acting chairman. I went very hurriedly to inform him of these developments. 'Don't worry, Moira,' he said. 'I shall simply say that it is not allowed for the relatives of members of staff to be employed.' And that, very neatly, put an end to Jack's plan – but I am still grateful that he offered me the job of development director.

Shortly after accepting it, I moved from the School building to a rather splendid office (not filled with gas) in the Foundation offices overlooking the High Street and I settled down to invent my job. There was nobody to tell me anything about it and there seemed to be nobody there who knew anything more than I did. Despite these rather obvious deficiencies, I somehow realised, right from the beginning, that this was exactly what I wanted to do and I was confident that I would be able to do it. The job was to fit me like a glove.

FUNDING THE ARTS

I was immediately faced with two separate tasks, each equally daunting. The first was to come to terms with the launch of the Aldeburgh Appeal and the second was to start finding commercial sponsors. As far as sponsorship was concerned the lack of guidance or a pattern to follow made a fundamental decision rather difficult. I had absolutely no idea what the cost of sponsoring a concert in the Festival should be and it felt a bit like the old game of Think of a Number. The problem was that there was no arts organisation in East Anglia of similar international prestige on which we could base our calculations and it was impossible to make comparisons with London sponsorships as our catchment area was entirely different and, in any case, and as I was to become horribly aware, half of it was in the North Sea. Another problem that had to be solved was what should be included in the sponsorship package.

In the course of learning as I went along, I made mistakes. The chief mistake I made was to decide to include the cost of entertaining the sponsor's guests in the package instead of charging for that element separately. I was later to see the folly of this but one of the reasons for an inclusive package was that I knew very well that our catering was not up to professional standards and, indeed, it was to remain a weakness for several years. George Gooderham, who was, after all, our landlord, insisted that he should supply all the catering himself, despite the fact that he had precious little catering experience and was certainly not a professional. There were disasters and I still go hot and cold when I remember some of them: finding that the chef had had a breakdown and simply hung up his coat and vanished; disbelief when I saw that George, anxious to please, had decided to give hungry, middle management guests only meringues and cream cakes; finding no food prepared and a poor little Suffolk girl in the prep room, concentrating hard and trying to string pearl onions and chunks of pineapple together – the list goes on and is the stuff of nightmares.

Despite his obvious shortcomings as a caterer and the headaches they gave me, George was always friendly and kind to me personally. Indeed, I always thought of him as a friend and I was very touched, when I left Aldeburgh, to be given by George a beautiful little watercolour of Snape – a picture I treasure and that hangs in my flat today.

A further problem was that we really had no space for entertaining and although we came up with a plan to hire a large marquee during the Festival, it was not an ideal solution. Our situation was rural, to say the least, and although concertgoers might have found a certain charm in old Victorian industrial buildings falling into disrepair, the paint peeling off them, and rutted, muddy roads to be manoeuvred in order to get to the car park, it was not exactly the situation one would choose when trying to attract sponsors.

I was aware of these limitations when I negotiated my first commercial sponsorship. I was told that Eastern Gas was anxious to expand its profile and that its directors might think that a Festival concert would provide the answer. Off went the letter and in due course I was invited to attend a meeting at their Potters Bar headquarters with their CEO, David Griffiths, and their marketing manager, Michael Switzer. I was taken on a grand tour of the building, which to my surprise I found fascinating; I had not realised that a decision had to be made each day as to how much gas was needed. It was slightly irritating to find that they rubbed their hands with glee when it was cold. After the tour we talked pleasantly and had lunch but I don't remember sponsorship being mentioned. A couple of weeks later, I was invited to meet the same people for lunch at a rather splendid restaurant. When the meal was finished, during which the conversation had been very friendly but no hint had been given about whether a deal would be reached, we were served coffee and the talk turned to sponsorship. Then David Griffiths asked the question I had been dreading, 'Tell me, Moira, how much will this cost us?' I tried to look and sound perfectly calm as I said as firmly as I could, 'Four thousand pounds.' 'Good,' he said. 'That is exactly what I had expected.' I was never more relieved and the figure I had decided on became the base from which we worked for all future sponsorships. In 2017, the equivalent figure would be £12,000.

One of the most important appointments that Jack Phipps had to make was that of concerts manager, a position that was currently vacant. He told me that he was looking at candidates and, as I was now a rather more senior member of staff, he wanted me to sit in on the interviews. He had trimmed the number of candidates down to two and in due course I was in his office for the first. I was not very happy when a young girl arrived wearing one of those long, droopy cotton dresses that always seem to have been trailed in mud, whatever the weather. The girl, whose long brown hair fell over her face, seemed to me to be as droopy as her dress but Jack was very enthusiastic about her and a fairly normal interview followed – normal compared to what was to come next.

A few days later the second candidate was due and, as he was working in London, it was possible for him to come to Aldeburgh only at lunch-time. The interview panel consisted of Jack, of course; Commander John

Jacob, the Treasurer; Peter Du Sautoy and myself. The plan was for all of us, including the candidate, to have a very quick lunch in Jack's office. Instead of sandwiches or something similar that could be eaten quickly and easily, for some unfathomable reason Jack chose steak, chips and salad. Steak is not the easiest thing to eat quickly while talking at the same time. The candidate was Kenneth Baird, then house manager at English National Opera, and he was in something of a rush as he had to get back to London on time in order to ensure that the auditorium was opened for the evening performance. I liked him immediately and my heart bled for him as he struggled manfully not to answer questions with a mouth full of steak. Jack did not appear to notice that there was anything unusual about the interview or that it put the candidate at a considerable disadvantage. So we all gobbled steak, trying both to talk and listen at the same time.

Later, without any discussion at all, Jack told me that he had decided to appoint the girl. 'Oh, please can't we have Kenneth Baird?' I said, rather rudely, but I was pleased that I had, as Sophie, as I think she was called, either could not take up the appointment or didn't want it and Ken, who was to go on to play such a crucial role in the history of the Aldeburgh Foundation, was appointed our concerts manager. It was certainly the best appointment that Jack ever made, although, as things were to turn out, perhaps he himself would not have agreed.

Meanwhile, I was still faced with launching a capital appeal. The target was £1 million, which might sound very little these days but in the early 1980s it was a large sum (the equivalent of more than £3 million today). Peter Bowring, highly respected in the insurance world, had accepted the chairmanship of the Aldeburgh Foundation and it would have been impossible to find a better person to fulfil the role. He had been involved with Aldeburgh and the activities at Snape since the earliest days, had a home in Suffolk and excellent contacts, but above all he was charming, likeable – and funny. He knew a great deal about fundraising in the City and, of course, was an obvious person to help with the Appeal.

However, the man who was to be the linchpin and chairman of the Appeal was Sir Richard Cave, known always as Dick Cave. He was at the peak of his career at this time, a leading industrialist, the chairman of Thorn EMI, deputy chairman of British Rail, and chairman of Vickers. His agreement to become the chairman of the Aldeburgh Appeal says everything about his generous nature and willingness to work for something he valued. Although at the time living in London, he had always had a home in Aldeburgh where he felt happiest and Suffolk was the county he loved. Dick Cave never did anything by halves and he threw himself completely into the task of getting the Appeal off the ground by forming a high-level committee. As the person who had to do the actual work, I valued Dick's help more than can be said. Probably one of the busiest men in England, he was always willing to give up his Saturday mornings to come to my office and go through the current situation – who to see, who to write to or telephone, all the activities for the following week.

The committee that Dick Cave formed consisted of:

David Barclay – Barclays Bank
Peter Bowring – Chairman, Aldeburgh Foundation
  and Chairman, C.T. Bowring
William Jacob – Aldeburgh Foundation Council member
Cyril Russell – lawyer and Aldeburgh resident
Sidney Spiro – banker (the husband of my great friend Diney Susskind)
Sir Peter Walters – Chairman, BP

I was listed as the secretary to the Appeal.

At the same time it was decided that while the committee would play an active role, there should also be a group of vice-presidents who would give the Appeal their support and allow their names to be listed as supporting the aims of the Appeal. It was certainly a star-studded collection of people:

The Right Reverend Faulkner Allison, formerly Bishop of Winchester
  and Aldeburgh resident
Peter Andry – record producer and Manager, EMI International Artists
Billy Burrell – legendary Aldeburgh fisherman, friend of Benjamin
  Britten and coxswain of the Aldeburgh lifeboat
Lord Delfont – Chairman and CEO, EMI Films and Theatre
  Corporation
Sir Kenneth Durham – Chairman, Unilever
Sir Peter Green – Chairman, Lloyds of London
Philip Greenwell – stockbroker

The Hon. Alan Hare – Chairman, *The Financial Times*
John Harvey Jones – Chairman, ICI
Andrew Lloyd Webber – composer
Sir Godfrey Messervy – Chairman, Lucas Industries
Sir Ian Morrow – management consultant
Richard Pears – relative of Peter Pears; Manager, Dairy Marketing
  Board
Sir Patrick Sergeant – City Editor, *Daily Mail*; President, Euromoney
Sir Gerald Thorley – Chairman, Allied Breweries
Sam Toy – Chairman, Ford Motor Company
Sir Ian Trethowan – Director-General, BBC

All this meant really hard work for me but I was happy and while I had to concentrate on the Appeal, finding sponsors for Festival concerts and other Foundation projects remained, of course, an important part of the brief.

We formed a very valuable relationship with Jaguar Cars, which became concert sponsors, while at the same time the company put together a series of events involving the Britten–Pears School in stately homes across the country. These comprised a concert performed by musicians drawn from the School, followed by what was described as a gourmet dinner, usually for about a hundred guests. We appointed a concert manager for the series, Heather Newill, and although I did not attend all the concerts, I did go to several of them, which meant visits to some of the most beautiful houses in the country. It proved to be a winning formula and Jaguar/Daimler sold their cars; our artists earned their fees; the School was paid, and everyone was happy. Indeed, so successful was the formula that it was expanded to three series and included events in Scotland and The Hague. It really is hardly surprising that the concerts were so successful. The first series was devised and presented by the inimitable Graham Johnson, who demanded the very highest standards not only from himself but from all the artists too. Sadly, he was too busy to undertake the following series of concerts but we were fortunate enough to persuade Iain Burnside to take charge of the future events. Iain has since done a great deal of presentation on television and radio and even in those early days it was obvious that he had a natural talent for charming the public. He was the ideal person to take on Graham's role as he had had a long connection with the School and had been a regular repetiteur on the courses, especially the French song course. He was a great admirer of Suzanne Danco, who, alongside Hugues Cuénod, directed the annual French song course.

A part of the deal with Jaguar was the sponsorship of a Festival concert and we arranged a floodlit display of their new cars outside the concert hall, seen by all the concertgoers as they arrived: an excellent opportunity for Jaguar and enjoyed by the concertgoers too. It was at one of these Jaguar-sponsored concerts that I became involved in a row that left me trembling and shaken for days afterwards. As all the catering was included in the sponsorship package, this had the result of the sponsor's guests mingling with not only the artists, which they loved, but also with any other Aldeburgh Foundation VIPs who naturally imagined that they had a perfect right to attend any of the receptions and who probably did not realise that it was actually the sponsor who was paying for all the food and drink.

On this dreadful occasion, I walked into the marquee after the concert to find that the Jaguar guests had not yet arrived and, while there were no other guests in the reception area, there was a young girl with two young men doing what I suppose you would call 'grazing'. They were walking about nonchalantly, where the food was set out, and enjoying an evening meal, helping themselves so enthusiastically that I feared that there would be noticeable gaps when the sponsor's guests arrived. I knew who they were. They were friends of a music publisher who had come down from London for the concert and she had obviously invited her friends to the concert.

Concerned for the Jaguar guests, I was absolutely furious and told the grazers to leave, but they were very cross and sulky and just hovered about glaring at me; short of manhandling them out, there was nothing I could do and they knew it. When Simon Rattle, the conductor of the concert, and Donald Mitchell walked in, I saw the three of them rush over to report what I had done. Then I saw rage descend on both Simon and Donald and when they reached me I really felt I might be vaporised by their anger. I shall never forget the fury in Simon Rattle's eyes as he said to me, 'Have you been rude to my guests?' I had to explain exactly what had happened and tell them – which I don't think they knew – that Jaguar was paying for the reception and that while all the artists were obviously most welcome, it was not a free-for-all. Eventually their anger diminished and both Simon and Donald seemed to understand. They were forgiving and afterwards it was forgotten but for me it was a truly awful moment and one that still has the power to make me feel positively ill.

FULL CITIZENSHIP

It was now that something happened very gradually, almost without my noticing, but I no longer felt as if I was in a foreign country; in fact, I had become a citizen. Snape Maltings Concert Hall, which to the rest of the world was one of the most important venues for classical and contemporary music, was so well known to me that it felt like my home. The most distinguished artists came to perform in the concert hall or to teach at the School and because of our unique circumstances I had the opportunity to know and to work with these musicians, several of whom were to become real friends. I found myself, through sheer good fortune, doing something I loved, in near-perfect circumstances. It was not only great musicians who were now part of my world but at the same time I was getting to know and trying to persuade the giants of the industrial and commercial world to support our cause. I could never ever have imagined that a time would come in my life when people such as Peter Pears, Nancy Evans and Eric Crozier would become friends, or that I would often be a guest at an informal lunch given by Mstislav Rostropovich and his wife Galina Vishnevskaya, and that such great privileges would feel absolutely normal. Nor would I ever have expected that, for instance, Sir Richard Cave would tell me to contact Sam Toy, then the Chairman of Ford UK, and find that I would be invited to have lunch with him at his offices to discuss the Aldeburgh Appeal. Given where I had started, it was all incredible but it had become my normal life.

Making friends with these stars had its unexpected side too. On one occasion I had invited Nancy Evans and Eric Crozier to dinner. I had also invited Stephen Ralls and Bruce Ubukata, two of the regular repetiteurs at the School; both of them were friends of Nancy and Eric and were great admirers of Nancy. The dinner went very well and everyone seemed happy. There was a lot of laughter and Nancy was at her best and funniest, regaling us with wonderful stories of her early career. I remember one particularly good story involved Kathleen Ferrier, who was a colleague and close friend of Nancy. Then I noticed that Eric was not speaking and that he had not spoken for some time, his mouth set in a tight, unforgiving straight line. I was not expecting what happened next, when he got up, left the table and left the house. Poor Eric, he loved Nancy but was so consumed by jealousy that he could not bear to watch her being admired, while nobody took much notice of him.

Another unforgettable story also involved Eric Crozier. At a Festival event, when I happened to be in the audience, he was giving a lecture in the Jubilee Hall on the subject of the libretto for *Billy Budd*, which he had written with E. M. Forster. He had a very clipped and precise form of delivery and always spoke in a strangled sort of voice, emphasising every vowel and every consonant. He was in full flow, before a very appreciative audience, when there was a series of very loud bangs backstage. It must be remembered that the Jubilee Hall really was the equivalent of the village hall and the arrangements backstage were primitive, to say the least. Between the actual stage and the back wall there was just a curtain and at the back of the building there was a large door that opened on to a roadway beside the beach. Our concerts manager, then Alastair Creamer, had to arrange for the delivery of a grand piano for an evening event and, forgetting Eric's lecture, had instructed the movers to bring it to the hall during the afternoon. So first of all, there was the sound of the door opening, loud noises as the movers tried to manoeuvre the piano into the backstage area, followed by very loud voices with strong Suffolk accents saying, 'Where do you want it, guv?' 'What, move it that way?' '*No* – not that way, over here.' Bang, bang, bang. I had to stuff a handkerchief into my mouth.

One of the teachers at the School with whom I became a real friend was Hugues Cuénod. As we had a French song course every year he taught regularly at the School. He was in his eighties when I first knew him. He lived until he was a hundred and eight, and he is in the *Guinness Book of Records* as being the oldest singer to make a debut performance at the Metropolitan Opera. Although in his earlier years he had sung in opera houses all over the world, it just happened that until he was eighty-four he had never performed at the Met. Hugues was one of the most charming people I have ever met and John Owen and I had the great good fortune of staying twice in his beautiful country house in Switzerland, a house built by his family in the mid-eighteenth century and never lived in by anyone else but the family. It was a slightly spooky house as it seemed as though nothing much had been updated since the eighteenth century, including the bathrooms and lavatories, but it really was beautiful, with the original silk wall hangings in the bedrooms.

When I was researching *Making Musicians* some years later, I went to visit Hugues, who was then a hundred and four, and living in his town house in Vevey. He was by then very frail and required constant care but he was perfectly able to answer questions and talk about his time at Aldeburgh. During the period of my research for the book, I also went to Moscow with Nick Winter, a fluent Russian speaker and a former Aldeburgh colleague, to visit Galina Vishnevskaya, of whom I had always been very fond.

Galina was in Aldeburgh, where she and Slava had a house, and teaching Russian song at the School when she was working on her wonderful memoir, every word of which she wrote herself. It was my job to pick her up in my car every day and take her to Snape. I would say something like 'What have you been doing?' and she would reply in her simple English, 'I write. I write. I tear up. I tear up.'

In 1984 both she and Slava were frequently in Aldeburgh. They were staying in their house in Paris, both addicted to watching the Los Angeles Olympics on television. Slava had an engagement to come to Aldeburgh, without Galya, and had apparently stayed up very late the night before watching television, which meant that he had to rush to catch the plane, get from Heathrow to Liverpool Street station and on to a train that would take him to Ipswich where Kenneth Baird had arranged to meet him and drive him to Aldeburgh. It was a Sunday. By the skin of his teeth, Rostropovich was on the train when there was one of those well-known announcements telling passengers that the train was not, after all, going to Ipswich but would stop at Manningtree and then proceed to Harwich. When the train got to Manningtree Slava was, predictably, fast asleep and made no move to get off. Fortunately a guard found him and in a great hurry helped Slava to climb out of the train with, as he described it, 'an enormous havvy suitcase' and then watched the train leave for Harwich. Only when he was on the platform did Slava realise that his millions of pounds' worth of cello was also on its way to Harwich. Here was this world-renowned cellist, whose English was fluent but heavily accented, alone on a platform at Manningtree station on a Sunday morning. Meanwhile, at Ipswich station a loudspeaker announced that Mr Kenneth Baird should go at once to the station master's office. There

Mstislav Rostropovich at the Britten–Pears School:
top Rehearsing with the Snape Maltings Training Orchestra (1978)
bottom left Taking a masterclass at the Jubilee Hall, Aldeburgh (1976)
bottom right Surrounded by students in the School foyer (1979)

Galina Vishnevskaya teaching on the 1981 Russian Song Course at the
Britten–Pears School – her students are Joan Rodgers and Hugh Mackey

top left Nancy Evans, Co-Director of Singing Studies, in 1979
top right Hugues Cuénod teaching on the 1982 French Song Course
below Regular accompanists for the School's singing courses:
Graham Johnson (*left*) and Stephen Ralls and Bruce Ubukata (*right*)

top Her Majesty The Queen Mother, Patron of the Aldeburgh Festival,
at the opening ceremony for the Britten–Pears School in 1979;
among those in attendance are Bill Servaes (*first left*), Sir Eugene Melville
(*third left*), Sir Peter Pears (*fourth left*), Pat Servaes, and Dr William Swinburne,
the first Director of Academic Studies at the School (*far right*)
below The Aldeburgh Appeal Concert at St James's Palace in 1983:
left Escorted by Sir Peter Pears, HM The Queen Mother meets
oboist Nicholas Daniel and Hugh Maguire
right Kenneth Baird and I are presented to Her Majesty

the station master – ashen-faced – said that there had been 'an accident' with Mr Rostropovich's cello at Manningtree station. Ken was to go there immediately but the station master did not give any specific reason. Slava had managed to explain his awful predicament to the Manningtree station master (how wonderful that there was one – these days there are only ticket machines at many country stations on a Sunday) who by a happy coincidence was an amateur cellist. By the time the station master had arranged for the cello to be secured at Harwich, he and Slava were engaged in a conversation discussing the merits of the E. J. Moeran cello concerto. Ken arrived to pick him up, drove him to Harwich to recover the cello and that night after the concert when Rostropovich was making a speech, he said, 'I have always loved certain cities – Paris, New York, London – but now I only love Manningtree.'

If the circumstances of my public life had changed so completely, it was as nothing compared to the changes in my head. I really did feel that I was a completely different person and the different person I had become was able to fit into the new life as though it had always been mine. It all felt right. The work, the friendships, the fun and laughter that seemed to be always there and, I suppose, the interest that every day seemed to bring, were what I had always wanted. Although I was so much older, my younger colleagues accepted me and I was included in everything that was happening. We treated Aldeburgh as though it was a suburb of London and would frequently drive to Ipswich after work, catch the train to London, go to the opera or to a concert and catch the last train back to Ipswich. On one occasion I was driving home from London and managed to get from the Aldwych to Aldeburgh in under two hours, which was driving very fast. The following day, when I told Peter Pears what I had done, instead of looking reproving and telling me that that was driving much too fast, he beamed and said, 'Well done.'

It is important not to forget that we were all there for only one reason and that reason was music. Whatever role we played in the organisation our only objective was to make music of the highest quality available to the thousands of concertgoers who flocked to the concert hall and to make sure that the School continued to encourage and nurture the careers of talented young musicians. Music was our raison d'être and we were immersed in it. As members of staff we were able to listen to some of the most sublime music in the world; we could attend concerts and sometimes slip in to a rehearsal. Added to this, if we were free we might be able to sit in on the most amazing masterclasses, watching extraordinary musicians teaching, perhaps going over and over one phrase until everybody could hear the difference. Sometimes one might observe the improvement that the whole course had made to a young singer's voice and this was exciting. When I think about it now, I realise just how lucky I was but, at the time, I'm afraid, it was sometimes taken for granted, just the background to our jobs. Yet even though it might have been taken for granted there was a part of me that knew it was miraculous and I felt a bit like dry ground after unexpected rain. It was so new and yet I felt that at last I was where I should always have been. I remember an occasion when Hugh Maguire said to me, 'You must have listened to an amazing amount of music, Moira', and it made me think and realise just what an amazing amount of music I had, indeed, heard. I felt that I had been offered a second chance.

CRISIS MANAGEMENT

It was now 1982 and our whole organisation was shaken by yet another huge change. Jack Phipps had been the general manager for just over a year and, although he must be given credit for his original and brilliant idea that became the enormously popular Snape Maltings Proms, his spending spree had reached such proportions that we were facing bankruptcy. Our Treasurer, John Jacob, was increasingly worried as the bills mounted and horrified when he discovered that Jack was concealing some of his more alarming spending from the Council, his employers. On one memorable occasion, our legal representative said at a meeting of the Council (which I now attended as a staff member) that unless something was done, we would have to cease trading. Dick Cave was, of course, now a Council member and at Council meetings he used to jingle the cash in his pocket when he was irritated; a rather scary amount of cash jingling went on during this period.

John Jacob was frequently in my office to discuss his concerns and finally one day I was told that there was to be an official enquiry and that Jack would be called to give evidence on his management of the Foundation. I was told that I would be required to attend the enquiry and as I was to be the only member of staff called to give evidence, I assumed that I would be asked to present a staff perspective. The day duly arrived, a Saturday, and we had an afternoon concert in the Maltings. I was told that the meeting would be held in the faculty room of the School and that I must be there at 2.30 p.m. As I arrived and walked into the School foyer an unrecognisable figure, bent almost double and clutching a briefcase to his chest, slunk past me, showing no sign of recognition. For a moment I genuinely did not know who it was and when I realised that it was Jack I was shocked; he normally had such a bouncy walk and such a bouncy manner that I could not help feeling sympathy for this broken figure sidling past me.

I was called into the faculty room to find a rather imposing panel, consisting of Peter Du Sautoy, Peter Bowring, Dick Cave, William Jacob, the brother of John and also a Council member, Rupert Rhymes, representing the Arts Council, and David Heckels, our legal representative, also a member of the Council. The atmosphere was friendly – apart from Rupert Rhymes, these were all people I knew quite well – and I was asked questions about the management, the running of the office and staff morale, all of which I answered frankly. I was then thanked and told I could go. Of course, I had no idea what was to happen and I went across to the concert hall and in at the back to sit on the management bench and listen to the performance. There was a wonderful secret entrance high up at the back of the hall, which led to a short flight of narrow stairs and at the top of the stairs, right at the very back of the hall, there was a bench where one could listen to the concert and come and go unnoticed.

Sitting there listening to the music, I was surprised when the door opened a crack and one of the front-of-house staff beckoned me to come out. 'They want you to go back to the enquiry,' she said. When I got to the faculty room, I was told by Peter Du Sautoy that it had been decided to terminate Jack's contract immediately but that they had not been able to reach a final decision about whom to appoint in his place and they needed to hear the opinion of someone giving a staff view. The two who were being considered were Kenneth Baird, our concerts manager, who having successfully eaten the steak at his interview, had now been with us for eight months, and John Jacob, the Treasurer. We all liked John. He and his brother, the sons of Sir Ian Jacob, formerly Director-General of the BBC, had both been members of the Council for many years, and John had become the Treasurer. Despite respect and even affection for John, I felt very strongly that he did not have the right qualities to take charge of the organisation, which, after all, was an important arts organisation, not just a trading business.

I said as emphatically as I could that in my view there really was no contest and that much as we all liked John, I thought that Kenneth Baird would be the better appointment. And so it was decided. I was asked if I knew how to contact Ken as he was away from Aldeburgh for the weekend and when I said that I did, I was told to ask him to return to Aldeburgh first thing the following morning. The reason for the urgency was that Peter Bowring was leaving for New York at 11 a.m. on that Sunday and it had been decided that he should dismiss Jack and appoint Ken before he left.

The following morning was like something out of a farce. I telephoned Ken and we agreed that he would come to my house at 9 a.m. and that we would then drive to Peter Bowring's house, which was outside Woodbridge, about a half-hour drive. Peter telephoned me early on Sunday morning and said that Jack was coming to see him at 8 a.m. and he thought that that would give him plenty of time to go through it all with Jack and be ready for us at 9.30, 'but just to be safe, I'll call you when he has left'. Just before nine the call came – 'the coast is clear' – and so when Ken arrived at nine we were able to set out immediately and I told him that he was about to be crowned. What none of us knew was that after taking his leave and on his way home, Jack decided to return, as he had thought of something that he believed might change the verdict. Now once you had driven through Woodbridge, the way to Peter's house was down a long narrow road with only just room for two cars to pass and pass with great difficulty; poor Peter was thrown into a potentially embarrassing situation with the clock ticking, an aeroplane to catch, Jack sitting there insisting that he, Peter, look at some figures, and Ken and me on our way. Peter knew it was too late to stop us; there were no such things as mobile phones then and so when he finally managed to persuade Jack as politely as possible but also as quickly as possible that there would be no change in the decision, he finally saw him off, with as he said, 'my heart beating very fast' and just hoping that the two cars were not going to meet and possibly collide.

Luckily, we didn't. Peter caught his flight and Kenneth Baird was appointed general manager of the Aldeburgh Foundation. It was the start of a wonderful period and it can be fairly said that Ken saved the situation, saved the whole Foundation. He re-negotiated a lucrative contract with the Central Electricity Generating Board who needed all the buildings at Snape to house the public enquiry into the desirability of a second nuclear power station at Sizewell, a couple of miles up the coast from Aldeburgh. Nowadays, it seems that the government just decides to have new nuclear power stations and that's that, but in the 1980s it meant a three-year, expensive public enquiry. The cash from the CEGB was a windfall that changed our situation but, in any event, Ken was a very successful manager who was respected by the staff; he ran not only a tight ship financially but the artistic programme was imaginative and well received by the audiences and the critics. Ken got on very well with Peter Pears and very well with the other core artistic directors, who included Oliver Knussen and Murray Perahia. He saw that John Owen was doing a good job with the School and, while supporting him in every way, left him to get on with it. Everyone was happy.

It was at this time that what we called the Monday Club was inaugurated. This was a regular meeting, usually late on a Monday afternoon, when Ken met with all the heads of department. These were John Jacob; John Owen; Virginia Caldwell, who had left the School staff to run the Aldeburgh Friends, a job for which she was particularly well suited and which she did extremely successfully; Perdita Hunt, now the director of the Watts Gallery and then our press and marketing manager; myself, and the new concerts manager, Alastair Creamer, who endured much leg-pulling and was told that he was technically not a member but was allowed to be present as the secretary. Today the original members of the Monday Club (sadly, without John Jacob and Virginia Caldwell who have died) meet for lunch once a year and have remained very good friends. All have gone on to have distinguished careers and because we all know each other so well and would all help each other, we have been dubbed the Aldeburgh mafia. Mafia or not, it is undeniable that we were all provided with an exceptional training ground.

BOB AND DORIS

I have not yet mentioned Bob and Doris Ling who played a prominent part in our lives. They were the concert hall caretakers and I don't think that there can be a person who was involved with either the hall or the School, from 1971, when they started work there, until their deaths in 2010 and 2011 less than four weeks apart, who would not have known Bob and Doris. Included would be all the international musicians, performers, conductors, teachers, students, broadcasters and the members of the Royal Family who came to Snape, particularly the Queen Mother and Prince Charles.

Bob and Doris were local people, he originally from Blaxhall, a rather strange village where the people firmly believe that stones grow, and she from Aldeburgh. They were childhood sweethearts and married in their teens; they were a devoted couple until their deaths when they had been married for nearly seventy years. Bob had started work at the maltings when just a boy and returned there after war-time service in the Royal Navy but, of course, eventually the maltings were sold and his employment ceased. Doris had been 'in service' more or less since childhood but now there were two children to feed and money had to be earned; with great initiative, they decided to become grave diggers.

With an old van and not much more than a couple of spades, they went grave digging over pretty well the whole of east Suffolk, she working just as hard as he did. Doris was a natural storyteller and I can well remember being helpless with laughter as she recounted being pulled backwards by an over-loaded wheelbarrow and ending up in the grave. After some years, they decided on a change – grave digging was hard and the money poor – and they took on a milk-delivery round. This proved to be far worse than grave digging. 'The inside of the van stank,' Bob said and they were constantly being bitten by small dogs.

They were living at Snape at the time, as were Britten and Pears, and Bob would say, 'I knew Ben. He would always stop and have a word with me when he was walking along by the river.' They had seen the concert hall built and then on that appalling night in 1969, the first night of the Festival, they had seen the whole thing burn down. (All concerned showed amazing determination, and the money was raised, the work commissioned, and, astonishingly, the rebuilt hall, with improvements, opened exactly one year later, in time for the 1970 Festival.) In 1971 Bob was told that there was a job going at the concert hall and, delighted by the prospect of an end to delivering milk, applied and was successful. Doris was included, as his assistant.

And so the final careers of these two remarkable people began. Bob, who knew nothing about classical music (although he was an adept on the mouth organ!), acquired exhaustive knowledge of setting the stage for whatever forces were performing and played an important backstage role in future opera productions. Doris, a very hard worker, enchanted everyone with her stories and her humour. 'Always cleaning them toilets,' as she used to say. I remember her telling me about the first time she was given gin and lime by some American airmen who were living in Snape. 'I had one,' she said. 'And then I had another. Well, we didn't know about things like gin and lime.' The end of the story was that, although they were living only a hundred yards away from the Americans' house, Bob had to fetch a wheelbarrow to get her home.

They both treated everyone in exactly the same way, whoever they were, and whether it was one of the kitchen staff, a world-famous conductor or a member of the Royal Family, they were just the same friendly and straightforward people. Prince Charles was a special fan of theirs and Ben and Peter loved them, as we all did. Towards the end of their lives, they were both unwell and Bob died in 2010 aged eighty-seven. There was a very emotional funeral in Aldeburgh Parish Church, which was packed to the rafters by their families, local people and mourners from London and beyond. Doris, heartbroken without Bob, died early in the new year.

THE ALDEBURGH APPEAL

Commercial sponsorship was always difficult at Aldeburgh. There was the charge of elitism and it is true that the profile of a company that did choose concert sponsorship would not be appreciably improved among the general public. It was a challenge, but we were reasonably successful and did number among our sponsors both Shell Oil and BP, the CEGB, two of the largest banks and various smaller commercial enterprises. Each year the target for sponsorship, rather frighteningly, became part of the budget, and each year I had to do my best to reach that target.

The Appeal took over a large amount of my time and effort and it was in 1983 that we were given permission to present a concert and dinner at St James's Palace in the presence of Aldeburgh's Patron, Queen Elizabeth, The Queen Mother, an event that would serve to launch the Appeal and, perhaps, to raise some money. This was entirely new territory for me and was the first of the many events with members of the Royal Family with which I was later to be involved. I was very green but the Queen Mother's

Household must have been used to people like me and I was given every possible bit of help. I was amazed when I was told that I did not have to submit the guest list to them: 'We trust you in this', which, in the event, proved to be rather worrying. We were inviting, I think, a hundred guests. It is not permissble to charge for such an event but the idea was to invite the good and the great, hoping that, when we wrote to them afterwards, asking for a donation, they would be generous.

In order to give the evening as much glamour as possible, we invited some stars, including Tom Conti and Paul Eddington along with their wives. Both these actors were currently appearing on television and were very well known; I thought they would seem rather exciting. We also invited Paul and Linda McCartney; it had occurred to me when I was doing the guest list that it would be fun to have one of the Beatles and I was pleased when they accepted the invitation. Two days before we were all due at the Palace, I nearly died of horror when the newspaper headlines screamed that Linda McCartney had been arrested at Heathrow for carrying drugs. She was on bail. Shaking a bit, I telephoned the person at St James's Palace who had been steering me through all the problems as they occurred, and told him that the McCartneys had been invited and accepted the invitation. What should I do? 'Well,' he said, 'that's rather unfortunate and all you can do is to try to keep their presence as low profile as possible.' 'Thank you very much. I'll do my best,' I said, wondering how on earth you keep the presence of Paul and Linda McCartney low profile.

The concert, which Hugh Maguire devised and in which William Pleeth and students from the School performed, went very well. The guests were then to move to the room in which the supper would be served, with the Queen Mother, her lady-in-waiting and a member of her Household standing at the entrance, when various people, all pre-selected, would be presented. It seemed to be going according to plan, when out of the corner of my eye, I saw the McCartneys approaching. Desperate thoughts rushed through my brain but I could hardly throw a blanket over their heads. Then I heard Queen Elizabeth say, delightedly, 'Oh, look, there's one of the Beatles', and motioned for them to come over to her. They stood chatting animatedly for some time and not just animatedly, for it seemed as if the Queen Mother was really enjoying herself. Perhaps it was a relief to talk to a Beatle rather than the approved guests who, in their conformity, were probably terribly boring.

Although the event was a great success, it did not bring in very much money. We wrote to everybody who had been present asking them to support our Appeal. After all, they had enjoyed a concert and supper at St James's Palace, with, let's not forget, one of the Beatles present. The response was pretty disappointing and it taught me a very valuable lesson: that this was a rotten formula for fundraising. Afterwards we put on various events for the Appeal. There was a performance of *Façade* at the Drapers' Hall and we were given one of the preview nights of *Starlight Express*, which allowed us to sell tickets at an inflated price.

One of our biggest fundraising efforts was the Aldeburgh Auction in 1985. It was decided that we would write to all those who had been involved with the Aldeburgh Festival and ask them whether they would donate a work of art or, in the case of composers, an original manuscript. Sotheby's agreed to host the auction. I think they were delighted to do so as it gave them the entrée to the Red House and allowed them to see Peter Pears's remarkable collection of contemporary art. With hindsight we realised that we had made an enormous mistake by selling the donated pictures and other works of art in the same sale as the music manuscripts. The buyers are very different people and we would have made a great deal more money if we had advertised and sold them separately. These are the lessons one learns.

There was great generosity and we were given some wonderful things. Peter Pears gave us a Constable cloud study, which was authenticated for the auction and fetched £26,000, a large amount in those days. Peter also donated sketches by Edward Lear, a watercolour by Boudin, a self-portrait by Gwen John and a bronze by Rodin. Sir Sidney Nolan gave us a remarkable drawing of a cellist and John Piper gave us his gouache and watercolour, *Lindisfarne Priory*, and Peggy Ashcroft donated a portrait of herself by Henry Lamb. It was my job to go to her house in Hampstead to collect it and I was somewhat surprised when she got down on the floor and fetched it out from under a sofa. 'I've always hated it,' she said.

Looking at the catalogue now I am absolutely astonished by the number of treasures, precious to their owners, that we were given. There were original letters from artists and composers and an autograph plan of Stravinsky's apartment in St Petersburg, works by Henry Moore, Elisabeth Frink and Mary Potter. Everything was of the highest distinction, including a case of Château Latour 1971 château-bottled

Pauillac! The Princess of Hesse and the Rhine, a long-time supporter of the Aldeburgh Festival, the Foundation's President and great personal friend of Britten and Pears, gave us an important diamond pendant, which was sold at a separate sale. As she has died and as it is so long ago, I think I may say this but at the time she wished the gift to be anonymous and it was described as being given by 'a lady of title who wishes to remain anonymous'.

The donations of original manuscripts were equally generous and included works by Stravinsky, Tippett, Ligeti and Lutosławski. None of them fetched what they would have in a dedicated manuscript sale but nevertheless the sale raised something in the region of £250,000, which was a very useful contribution to the Appeal. I don't like to imagine what these works of art and manuscripts would bring in if they were sold today. All one can say is that the buyers at the Aldeburgh Auction made very good investments.

One memorable story connected to the Auction concerned the visit of the head of Sotheby's music manuscript department, Dr Stephen Roe, who came to discuss some of our donations with Peter Pears at the Red House. When the meeting ended Peter, who after his stroke was partially paralysed, pointed with his stick to an ornament placed on a high shelf in his study. It was a bird, an avocet, and at the time Peter was always thinking about the Auction and deciding what he would give and he liked to have an idea of the value of possible donations. Pointing to the bird he said to Stephen Roe, 'I wonder if you would tell me about the avocet? Perhaps you could get it down?' Stephen Roe looked up nervously at the bird, obviously wondering what on earth to say. 'Um . . . it's not really my area of expertise, Sir Peter.' 'Well, get it down and we can look at it.' The next thing poor Stephen Roe knew was that he had to climb up on top of Peter's desk, tottering slightly and now very nervous, as he handed down the avocet to Peter. Kenneth Baird and I arrived in the middle of the exercise and found it hard to keep straight faces but I think Peter finally accepted that it really wasn't Dr Roe's area of expertise.

The Auction was tremendously exciting. Things were going reasonably well and I was learning a lot very quickly. It was at this time that I began my American visits. The Aldeburgh Festival, since its very early days, had been supported by a group of high-flyers in the American music world and their support, which was not only financial, had always been very important. Now their chief role was focused on raising money for bursaries to support the many American students who wanted to study at the School. Historically there had always been difficulties between the two organisations with accusation and counter-accusation, mainly concerned with the exchange of information and, perhaps, a feeling never expressed, that the Brits were always begging for money. The archive at the Red House is filled with letters dealing with these problems. At one time Bill Servaes and Pat, his wife, had gone to New York especially to try to pour oil on these troubled waters.

I think that it was inevitable that when we started our own fundraising efforts, the problems would only increase and they became the subject of endless debate. As a result of these discussions it was decided that I should undertake a sort of American tour, liaising with our American Friends organisation in New York, but also hoping to raise money from other independent sources. Dick Cave arranged for me to stay with a Mexican widow, whose husband had been his friend, in her wonderful Park Avenue apartment. She had never seen me before in her life but I received the warmest welcome one can imagine from Beatriz Nisonger, and she has remained a friend. I was very thankful that my stay with her was such a success because nothing else went quite the way I had hoped. I attended a meeting of the Board of the American Friends and they were all polite but I felt that my visit did nothing to alleviate any of the suspicions that they nursed.

My travels within the US were not much more successful. In Minneapolis I visited Philip Brunelle, the American conductor who had brought the cast of *Paul Bunyan* to the Festival; Dr Melvin George in Columbus, Ohio; a very grand old lady in Dallas, and Colin Graham, still an artistic director of the Aldeburgh Festival in name, and now living in St Louis. It was utterly exhausting. I stayed in really horrible hotels and moved from one airport to another in a sort of daze. Everyone was kind and supportive but there was not much actual money raised and I felt a sense of failure. Altogether I made four visits to the United States while working for Aldeburgh, staying once in New York in a flat loaned to me by Elmer Bernstein, the film music composer who had become a friend after directing a film music course at Snape in 1980. I stayed twice with Dedie and De Witt Horner, who were also friends of Dick Cave, and who, like Beatriz Nisonger, welcomed me as though it was I who was their old friend.

One of these visits was arranged by Jim and Fran Laurence. Jim was the President of the Boston branch of the English Speaking Union and he was an enthusiastic supporter of the School, raising money that was to be spent on ESU bursaries for American students. On one of his visits to Snape we discussed the idea of making a 'film' about the School that he wanted me to show to an ESU audience in Boston. The result of this initiative was a slide show which was put together by a professional firm in Ipswich. It seems strange to think that there were no such things as videos then and the best that we could do was this heavy carousel with slides, each one dropping into place as the carousel went round. Peter Pears made the commentary to go with the show and as music we chose the *Sea Interludes* from Britten's *Peter Grimes* – to this day I can never hear that music, which I know so well, without my stomach churning.

An itinerary was produced and I was to show the slides to audiences in New York, Boston and Toronto. With courage born of ignorance, I set out, armed with the carousel, which I could not let out of my sight. My aim was to enthuse audiences about the benefits of supporting the School and for them to provide the means for more North American students to study there. My first stop was New York and a hall had been booked, the audience invited and a technical assistant on hand to help with the installation of the slide show. We were met with immediate problems as the electrical impulse on the carousel was at variance with the New York electrical supply, necessitating hours of trial and error, until we got it right. I should have been warned, but in the end it went quite well and I was pleased.

The next stop was Boston and I stayed with the Laurences in their beautiful Brookline house. Jim was an architect and had built a modern house on land belonging to his family and made a stunning Japanese garden; he was a very distinguished Bostonian, one time chairman of the Boston Symphony Orchestra and chairman of the Eliot Gardner Museum. I knew how essential it was to have a technical assistant on hand and the show went reasonably well. I went on to Toronto, under the kindly auspices of Marshall and Françoise Sutton, who were regular visitors to the Aldeburgh Festival. Françoise was the chairman of the Canadian Friends of the Aldeburgh Festival and a tireless fundraiser of bursaries for Canadian students. I knew them both quite well and was a friend and admirer of Françoise – very French, always elegant and charming.

I was told that I was *honoured* as the Arts Club of Toronto would hold a lunch for invited guests and that the slides would be shown in the very grand Club premises. I can't now remember why it was all such an *honour*, perhaps because women were not normally allowed into these hallowed premises or perhaps because women were not normally allowed to raise their voices and I would, of course, be giving a talk. Whatever the reason was, it was made clear to me that indeed it was an *honour*. Again, I had to make certain of the presence of the technical assistant and spent some time in the morning going through the slides and ironing out the technical difficulties, of which there seemed to be rather a lot. The assistant was very confident and I left to go to the lunch feeling more or less happy.

We all lunched at tables of six and I have absolutely no memory at all of the lunch or who my table companions were. Eventually I had to stand up, conquer my nerves and make a speech about the School and the value that Canadians had derived from studying there. I got through it all without a hitch and then said, as usual, 'Shall we see the slides now . . .?' The familiar *Sea Interlude* music started, a slide came on to the screen and instead of Peter Pears's beautiful speaking voice, out came gobbledegook. Loud gobbledegook. I don't think anyone has ever run faster. I positively sprinted to the little alcove where the carousel and the technical man were. I was not encouraged when, in answer to my hissed, very rude, question, he said, 'I really don't know.' I've had some awful moments and this was certainly one of them. In any event, the problem was eventually fixed, the slides were shown to polite applause and I was very unhappy about it.

BILL

Back in Aldeburgh, life and work continued as usual but 1986 was to be a milestone in my life. In January, my youngest son Julian married Polly Browne, a marriage that has now lasted for nearly thirty years. At the time, I was against his marrying because I felt that he was much too young (not quite twenty-four), but thankfully I was wrong and if proof were needed of how wrong I was, my grandsons, Oliver and Tom, provide the evidence. In March I was in Cookham, spending the weekend with them and on my return on Sunday afternoon, a young policeman came to my door to tell me that my beloved son Bill had died.

Even after all these years it is difficult to write about it. Bill was a heroin addict and from what I know, it seems almost inevitable that one day there will be overdose. The fact that a young man's life is ruined by drugs is very hard to live with: all the false hopes, all the promises, the pleading, the tears shed and, above all, the knowledge that the person himself longs, above all, to lead a different life, and doesn't know how to. To so many people drug addiction is something pretty despicable, not worthy of sympathy, and to them a drug addict is essentially a worthless person. This makes the circumstances even harder to bear – you long to shake these smug judges who seem to know so very little. Bill had always been a popular and well-liked person and the fact that so many of his friends were there in that awful, soulless crematorium was a comfort at a very comfortless time. Diney Spiro (formerly Susskind), my dear old friend, was kind and invited all those present to her flat in Marloes Road for a drink and a sandwich. This was a comfort, too.

Bill died on 23 March and on 3 April Peter Pears died. I shall never forget standing in Aldeburgh Parish Church graveyard on one of those awful east-coast days of miserable rain and wind, for the funeral of the singer, who had become a friend. There was grief on every face and life did feel very cold. Kenneth Baird was very kind to me, and would not have minded if I had stayed at home for a while, but I found that working was by far the best thing to do and I told him that I was happy to continue with plans that we had made for me to undertake another American visit. Peter's funeral was on the 9th and on 11 April I flew to New York and stayed, once again, with the De Witt Horners who had been so generous with their hospitality. The reason for my visit was to put the finishing touches to plans for a visit to London for wealthy Americans, which would include another reception at St James's Palace in the presence of the Queen Mother.

FURTHER ROYAL PATRONAGE

I was in the US for ten days and then we were all swept into the arrangements for a memorial concert for Peter and his memorial service in Westminster Abbey. Rosamund Strode, who had worked for Britten for years and after his death continued to perform a very important role at the Britten–Pears Library, was in charge of all the seating plans for the Abbey for the memorial service. Westminster Abbey was absolutely packed and I was immensely honoured to find that she put me in one of the choir stalls, which meant that I had a perfect, unobstructed view of the whole service, which was beautiful and very moving. Ken was not so pleased with me and says that I caused him one of the most embarrassing moments of his life. When we arrived a verger wanted to know where we had been placed and I said, about Ken, 'This is the general manager of the Aldeburgh Foundation.' 'Oh,' he said. 'Madam, will you please go down that aisle to your seat, and, sir, if you would wait a moment for me.' The verger returned with his silver rod of office. 'Please sir, will you follow me?' Very slowly he proceeded to process down the central aisle of the Abbey, followed by Ken, who said he found it a very, very long walk and that he had never ever felt so exposed or embarrassed.

Of course, a memorial concert was an immediate priority and there was much talk about where it would take place and what form it would take. Prue Penn and Marion Thorpe agreed to become joint chairmen of a concert committee, which would help sell the tickets and raise funds for the Appeal. Prue is the extremely beautiful widow of Sir Eric Penn, a member of the Royal Household, and at that time they lived at Sternfield, near Aldeburgh, a very fine house, where they were endlessly hospitable in that generous and apparently effortless manner that usually means there has been a great deal of work behind the scenes. Prue loved the Festival and had been a great friend of both Ben and Peter and always a keen supporter of all our activities. Marion Thorpe, a gifted pianist, was the daughter of Erwin Stein, a friend of Britten, and had been involved with the Aldeburgh Festival from its earliest beginnings. She had been married to the Earl of Harewood and, after their divorce, married Jeremy Thorpe, the Liberal politician. The Thorpes had a house near Aldeburgh and Marion had been a close friend of Britten and Pears since the Second World War; the Thorpes were very keen supporters of not only the Festival but of all the other activities that took place at Snape, including the School.

We could not have had better chairmen and I was confident that their committee would sell tickets for the gala concert with ease. I think that everybody had envisaged the normal format for a memorial concert but the artistic directors had decided that there would be a performance of Britten's *War Requiem* in the Royal Opera House. It was a bit unusual, to say the least, and a surprise when Ken discovered that Paul Findlay,

Manager of the ROH, imagined that we would be able to mount a performance of *War Requiem* using only the forestage over the orchestra pit – a misapprehension that Prue helped change. Alastair Creamer, concert manager, when being shown where all the dressing rooms were and discussing who would be occupying each room, was equally taken aback when Trevor Jones, the house manager, opened a door where one of the artists would be dressing, only to find that it was a cupboard.

In the event it was all a huge success, with HRH Princess Alexandra the guest of honour. Galina Vishnevskaya, Anthony Rolfe Johnson and John Shirley-Quirk were the soloists in *War Requiem* and Anne-Sophie Mutter with Bruno Giuranna performed Mozart's Sinfonia concertante. Simon Rattle was the conductor with the City of Birmingham Symphony Orchestra and CBSO Chorus. It was a very distinguished, stylish occasion and, of course, warmly received. Despite its enormous success, I had cause to be infuriated twice that evening. The first was when I spoke to Sir Edward Heath, sulking in a corner, and he said of *War Requiem*, 'It's a rotten piece.' As an invited guest I thought he was extremely rude. The second was at the very end when I decided that I deserved a drink and asked for a glass of champagne. 'Sorry, madam, the champagne is finished' was the response from the barman. He had no idea who I was but as I had been in charge of the catering, I knew that this could not possibly be true and I told him so. A bottle immediately appeared and I was cross to think that the bar staff were simply helping themselves to the champagne and imagined how embarrassing it would have been if one of our guests had been refused a drink.

The visit of the Americans passed off well but might very well not have. Queen Elizabeth The Queen Mother, then in her nineties, suffered from a much publicised ulcer on her leg and was forced to go into hospital. The Americans had been attracted to the event on the understanding that the Queen Mother would be present and it seemed that she might very well be unable to attend. I was well aware that it would be virtually impossible to arrange for another senior member of the Royal Family to attend at such short notice and I was very anxious. But the wonderful Queen Mother was indeed there, dressed in a beautiful green chiffon dress, with the bandage on her leg starting to unwind. We had a string quartet, the Brindisi Quartet, who had all attended the Britten–Pears School, playing in the bay of a window. I was there in a strictly working capacity but at one moment when there was a break in the business of presenting guests to Her Majesty, she said to me, 'Let's go and listen to the musicians.' We walked to a little table with two chairs and sat there listening to the music. I felt like saying, 'I'm just a slave here and really you should be with some of the important people', but that would not have done and so I sat there quietly chatting to our wonderfully charming Queen Mother, enjoying every moment, and feeling like an imposter about to be exposed.

In 1986 there was to be another tragedy. Poor Dick Cave had been battling a brain tumour with great courage but in early December he died. Lord Jellicoe, a close friend of Dick, gave the address at his funeral in Aldeburgh Parish Church and Gilly, Dick's widow, chose 'Che farò senza Euridice?' from Gluck's *Orfeo ed Euridice* to be sung by a student from the School. It was all desperately sad and I felt that I had lost a true friend.

I spent Christmas with my old friends the Gibsons, who were more like family than friends. He was the vicar of Badminton and lived in the beautiful Badminton vicarage, which I knew well and where I had stayed many times previously. Soon 1986 became 1987 and I had no idea that, again, my life was to change dramatically.

In the summer I was telephoned by Henry Wrong, managing director of the Barbican Centre in London, inviting me to have lunch with him. He told me that the Barbican had hitherto used agents to raise sponsorship but now he had decided to open a sponsorship department and offered me the job of heading it up. I was utterly astonished, flattered and frightened by the enormous decision I had to make. I had always imagined that I would remain in my Aldeburgh job, which I loved, until I stopped working. In fact, it proved to be an easy decision to make. I knew that if I said no, I would always wonder what it would have been like to work in London and that it was rather feeble to be too afraid and stay for ever with the known and familiar. And so I accepted the offer and arranged to start in December.

There was sadness involved in this, too, and I knew how much I would miss my colleagues, especially Kenneth Baird with whom I so enjoyed working and who had become such a friend. The next months were very busy. I sold my house in Aldeburgh, bought a flat in Clapham, went to Australia to see my son David, who had been away from home for such a long time and was now married with two daughters. Then I prepared myself for the challenge of London.

LONDON AND AFTER

HENRY WRONG WELCOMED ME warmly and showed me the large, rather splendid office that would be mine. Having spent years recovering from my initial self-doubt at Aldeburgh, I now found myself once again in its familiar grip. It was one thing to be head of development at Aldeburgh, something I had become so used to, but quite another to take on London, in a job within an enormous organisation. (The Barbican Centre was itself part of an even larger organisation, the Corporation of London.) I started a month before my sixty-third birthday and I kept thinking what an idiot I had been to imagine that I could make this a success and how stupid to subject myself once again to anxiety and the awful feeling of inadequacy. The twice-daily drive from Clapham to the Barbican in rush-hour traffic was frightening enough, but things felt worse after meeting all the Barbican heads of departments with whom I would be working; arts, finance, marketing, press and public relations, security, maintenance, conference and exhibitions, personnel – the list seemed endless and very different from the small, friendly and informal administration at Aldeburgh. The actual process of seeking sponsorship, the reason I was there, didn't even bear thinking about, but as in my first days of working for the Britten–Pears School, I knew that I was here and I just had to get on with it.

The very first hurdle was the question of a secretary. In those pre-computer days a secretary was essential and the personnel department of the Barbican was instructed to send me candidates for interview. Knowing how many young people wanted to work in the arts, I expected that there would be plenty of suitable applicants. I was very surprised that there seemed to be only a trickle and that each one was worse than the one before. Finally, I discovered that the job had been advertised only in some internal Corporation of London publication and this had obviously not produced anyone who fitted the bill. There clearly was an assumption that secretarial posts would be taken by women: somewhat exasperated with the people I had seen, I asked the head of personnel whether any young men ever wanted to do this sort of work at the Barbican? 'Well,' she replied, 'we have had an application from a young man, but he is not a secretary.' I told her I didn't care about that, believing that any intelligent person could learn to type and do the filing in no time at all, and asked to see him.

The next day Colin McKenzie walked into my office and not only into the job but into the rest of my life as one of my closest and most important friends. He was twenty-two at the time, had recently graduated in art history from Sussex University; this would be his first job. I saw his enthusiasm and his bright, intelligent eyes and knew at once that here was the secretary that I had hoped to find. Immensely personable, he became a very popular member of staff and was especially well liked by Henry Wrong, who got into the habit of coming into the office, which I now shared with Colin, to have a morning cup of coffee, which Colin made each day in the filter machine I had decided to buy.

IMAGES DE FRANCE

The Arts Department, headed by Antony Lewis-Crosby, had several sub-divisions and all of them seemed to need sponsorship. My job was to help them get it. However, in 1988, there was to be one huge and important festival, involving all sections of the Barbican Centre, and this took foremost place in our planning. This was the French festival entitled 'Images de France', the total cost of which would be enormous, with the sponsorship requirement equally enormous. In fact, to someone with only my somewhat limited experience of fundraising, the amount was staggering. The sum of £250,000 was needed more or less immediately.

I was incredibly fortunate. Elisabeth Maxwell, the wife of Robert Maxwell, the controversial publisher and media proprietor, was the chairman of the festival committee and I was told that she wanted me to make an appointment with the representatives of Eurotunnel. At this point I had not met her but over the months of working with Elisabeth Maxwell I grew to admire her enormously and I became very friendly with her. She was a remarkable woman who loved Robert Maxwell and her family with complete selfless devotion.

128

IMAGES DE

FRANCE

A CELEBRATION OF 300 YEARS OF FRENCH CULTURE · VISUAL ARTS · MUSIC · FILMS · SPECIAL EVENTS

12 MAY - 17 JULY 1988 · BARBICAN CENTRE

EURO TUNNEL

"IMAGES DE FRANCE" IS ORGANISED BY THE BARBICAN CENTRE WITH THE
CO-OPERATION OF L'ASSOCIATION FRANCAISE D'ACTION ARTISTIQUE, MINISTERE DES
AFFAIRES ETRANGERES A PARIS WITH FINANCIAL SUPPORT FROM EUROTUNNEL.

On one occasion I was talking to her about the death of her eldest son. As a young man he had been involved in a car accident, which had left him in a coma, unable to communicate in any way. He was in this state for seven years before his death, and for seven years his mother visited him every day. 'I couldn't bear to think that one day he might wake up and that I would not be with him.' She also told me, when we were talking about her having eight children, 'I wanted to have a large family for Bob. He had lost all his family in the Holocaust and he was so alone. I wanted to give him a real family again.' I enjoyed our conversations and I began to feel that it was a privilege to work with her.

As far as the meeting with Eurotunnel was concerned, I had long discussions with Antony Lewis-Crosby, about what could be included in the sponsorship and what we could offer. Then, having done as much homework on the company as I could, I went to the Eurotunnel offices, reasonably optimistic in the knowledge that, in the way these things work, the decision-makers there had already been softened up by Robert Maxwell at the instigation of his wife. This was before the opening of the Channel Tunnel, which had been plagued by endless, very expensive, problems and by acrimonious disagreements between the French and the British companies. Many people at this time thought that the tunnel might never be completed. All the difficulties of the project had been extensively aired in the press and, with problems between the French and British governments added to the mix, it really did seem as though it might all end in failure. In these difficult circumstances this was a perfect sponsorship opportunity for Eurotunnel, a high-profile multi-media event in the centre of London, celebrating French arts and culture.

I had another stroke of luck. The British chief executive of Eurotunnel was Alastair Morton, who was a South African and whose family I knew very well. I had no idea that I was going to see him at that first meeting but we were soon talking about Tim Cullinan, my friend Lovelle's younger brother, whom I had known all his life and who was a great friend of Alastair. Although links such as these would not alone have persuaded him to back us, they certainly oiled the wheels. I had been told that Morton had a reputation for being off-hand and distant, but the meeting could hardly have gone better. The only fly in the ointment was the Eurotunnel PR lady whose name I forget, but we took to calling her 'Jaws'. The name stuck and I recall Henry Wrong saying quite naturally to me on one occasion, 'Have you got a telephone number for Jaws, Moira?'

When I think about the extraordinary achievements of Alastair Morton – without him the tunnel might not have been built and would certainly have taken very much longer to reach completion – I am struck by the number of South Africans and Rhodesians/Zimbabweans who have left Africa and made such significant contributions to European life. In the arts one thinks immediately of actors Sir Antony Sher and Dame Janet Suzman, playwright Sir Ronald Harwood and the sculptor Stella Shawzin. In the law there is Lord Hoffmann the retired senior Appeal Court judge and in medicine and science there is Sir Raymond Hoffenberg, a well-known anti-apartheid activist who became President of the Royal College of Physicians and President of Wolfson College, Oxford. Tony Bloom is a leading light in the London business world and a generous benefactor of the London Symphony Orchestra; Henry Meakin, a Zimbabwean, founded Classic FM and Prue Leith is a remarkable restaurateur and cookery writer. The list goes on and on and even J.R.R. Tolkien was born and brought up in South Africa! I am listing only white South Africans and marvelling that such a tiny population could produce such luminaries, but black South Africans, too, have made their mark in Britain. With apartheid a generation behind us, this will happen more and more, especially, I think, in the arts. In Johannesburg and Cape Town now there is a very lively arts scene, entirely different from the days when I lived in South Africa.

Despite Jaws's fierce demands and insistence on every detail being examined and approved (by her), I was enormously relieved and thrilled when at the end of this first meeting with representatives from Eurotunnel Alastair Morton simply asked, 'How much are you looking for?' 'Two hundred and fifty thousand pounds,' I replied, and he said, 'Well, you can have it.' When I got out of the taxi on my return to the Barbican, I was met by Antony Lewis-Crosby who asked, very anxiously, 'Have you got it?' I was suddenly very tired and just answered, 'Yes.' 'But how much of it have you got?' 'All of it.' I don't think I have ever seen anybody so delighted. It was a coup, but I felt that it had had very little to do with me. Over the months of preparing for the opening of the festival, Jaws mellowed a lot and in the end we were all quite fond of her.

Eurotunnel was the major, overall sponsor of Images de France but individual concerts and exhibitions were available for sponsorship and required money; consequently the first months of 1988 were very hectic. It was also complicated. The Royal Shakespeare Company and the London Symphony Orchestra were tenants and resident companies, but their managements were entirely independent. This meant that, for example, LSO concerts were sponsored through the LSO administration, but because we all worked so closely together, I was able to offer sponsors LSO concerts that were a part of Images de France, if I had the orchestra's approval.

It was proposed that everything in the centre would reflect the festival: the restaurants were to serve French food, which seemed to mean croissants in the mornings and not very much else; the shop planned to sell French products, and the Eurotunnel logo had to be seen throughout the whole building. Our main exhibition area was devoted to installations by prestigious, contemporary French artists. I still don't understand installations and I remember watching one of the French artists spending hours over his particular offering, which comprised three wooden boxes filled with what looked like pumpkins, butternut squash and various gourds. Each of these was placed very, very carefully, all having been brought especially from France. In the end it looked to me like any old wooden boxes outside a greengrocer's. There were also light boxes on the floor, each one showing pictures of the sky, blue with white clouds moving very, very slowly. These, too, were positioned with extreme care. I did not express any opinions.

Apart from trying to find sponsors for the individual events, I remember spending endless hours in meetings with the marketing department, with the press and PR department, the caterers, and the designers who had been contracted to come up with an overall design for the foyers and public spaces. There seemed to be no end to meetings and the demands of Jaws were always in evidence. There were also meetings and receptions at the French Embassy and the cultural attaché went out of his way to help – especially to help me in the search for sponsorship. As far as the overall design was concerned, I was rather disappointed and I did not think that it justified the expense of professional designers. There were Eurotunnel logos everywhere and that was about it. The idea was that visitors to the centre would feel that they had somehow, miraculously, been transported to France, but I thought it didn't quite come off.

The Barbican Centre, London
top left An aerial view   *top right* The foyer light sculpture
bottom The lakeside open-air restaurant

Opening Night: Anthony Camden, principal oboist of the LSO
and the orchestra's chairman, is presented to Her Majesty The Queen
by Henry Wrong (*top*), and the concert hall (*below*)

top Henry Wrong inspects progress on the construction of the hall
bottom left During the *Daily Mail*-sponsored trip to Budapest related to the
Magyarok festival, I meet an accordionist
bottom right Colin McKenzie

top left Her Majesty The Queen visits the Barbican, escorted by Henry Wrong
top right Diana, Princess of Wales, at an LSO reception, with Mr Yamataka
bottom left Henry Wrong, with Anthony Camden, prepares to cut the cake
at the Barbican's fifth birthday celebrations
bottom right Elisabeth Maxwell

In addition to the meetings, I remember receptions and parties, one of which took place at the Savoy. It was my first introduction to Robert Maxwell and I immediately understood why so many were in thrall to him. He had enormous charm when he chose to show it and on this occasion he took my hand in both of his and said, 'I've heard all about you', all the time looking at me very intently. The charm rather failed when he left the Savoy quite abruptly, leaving his poor wife not knowing that he had gone.

He displayed even greater lack of charm on another rather more important occasion. A prestigious event of the festival was an LSO concert which the Queen Mother was attending; all the good and the great had been invited. The Maxwells were hosting a post-concert dinner at which just a few guests were to be present.

The concert started and, as Elisabeth Maxwell was the chairman of the festival committee, the Maxwells had been placed in prominent seats in the front row of the circle, beside the Queen Mother. Robert Maxwell had been present at the reception before the concert, and had looked as though he was following the royal party into the hall, but suddenly turned on his heel and left. His absence meant that a front row seat was empty, which was obviously an embarrassment for Elisabeth; fortunately Henry Wrong covered it up very well. Robert Maxwell, however, was not only absent from the concert, but failed to arrive for the post-concert dinner that he and Elisabeth were hosting.

Among the select few who were invited to both the concert and the dinner were the Duke and Duchess of Buccleuch, whose seats for the concert happened to be just in front of mine. About half an hour before the concert started someone came up to me and said, 'Moira, you do know, don't you, that the Duke of Buccleuch is in a wheelchair?' I thought I might faint. Colin was summoned, looking very smart in his dinner jacket, and was told that he would have to meet the duke and conduct him to the place in the hall dedicated to wheelchair users.

At that time the facilities for disabled people in the Barbican Centre were not satisfactory, to say the least, and in this case, involved a diversion through the backstage area. Poor Colin, with tremendous elan, escorted the duke, but found that when he got backstage there was a hitch, which meant a delay of at least twenty minutes. I was so proud that he coped with this, with no difficulty at all, and stood chatting to the duke for the entire time. Afterwards the duke thanked us for the way he had been cared for and remarked especially on Colin's charm.

Finally Images de France came to an end and in many ways the festival had been a great success. No sooner was it finished, than we started planning for the 1989 international festival which was to be Hungarian. The background to this period was disconcerting. Having been involved in some of the movement to get rid of Jack Phipps at Aldeburgh, I now found, to my dismay, that there were very serious plotters at the Barbican. I wanted nothing to do with them and I felt very strongly that it all had nothing to do with me. Apart from anything else, I was Henry Wrong's appointee and I owed all my loyalty to him.

The leading plotter was one of the most senior officials whom I happened to like personally, and whose intelligence I admired very much. He often came into my office for an informal chat and it was quite some time before the penny dropped, and I realised just what he was doing. For some reason, he had decided that he wanted me to join him in the plot and although I perfectly understood the background to his thinking, I wanted to have no part whatsoever in it. In the circumstances, it was a fine line to tread, especially as I was still fairly new to the job and I knew that not only was he clever, but also that he was determined and quite ruthless. Just how ruthless, I learned only afterwards when I discovered that he had had skeleton keys to the safe made. What he did achieve as a first step was to persuade the Corporation of London Barbican Committee, who were our masters, to instigate a complete survey into the management of the centre. This was to be undertaken by an independent consultant.

In due course the consultant, Clive Priestley, a former senior civil servant, arrived and we were told that he would be visiting every department and taking evidence from every head of department. He had a rather snake-like appearance, with cold eyes, and he had the extraordinary ability to write notes while conducting an interview, at the same time never taking his eyes off the face of the person to whom he was talking. I was fascinated by this trick and longed to ask him how he did it. But I was far too busy concentrating as I was very scared of being trapped into saying something that I would regret.

This, then, was the background to the planning of the Hungarian festival. The artistic director of the festival was to be Hans Landesmann. It was considered a great feather in our cap to have him involved in the festival, especially as he brought extensive knowledge of Hungarian contemporary music to the project. The son of a wealthy Jewish family of wholesale meat traders, he had studied the piano himself and after the family was forced to flee, he obtained a doctorate in chemistry at the Sorbonne. He struck me as a very vain man and I got the feeling that he wanted to run the whole show himself, and rather resented the fact that there were other interests involved. He certainly showed absolutely no sympathy for the fact that money was needed and that it was my job to get it. However, he did come up with a very good name for the festival – reverting to Hungarian – which was to be called 'Magyarok'.

One of the people Henry Wrong approached when we started looking for support was Vere Rothermere, Viscount Rothermere, who was chairman of Associated Newspapers and happened to have a particular connection with Hungary. In 1927, seven after the Treaty of Trianon, the first Lord Rothermere declared his passionate support for the Hungarian cause. Although this sentiment was rumoured to have been inspired by his affection for a famous Hungarian aristocratic beauty, his support was nevertheless received with wild enthusiasm by the Hungarians. In fact, it was suggested that he should be offered the throne, which was vacant at the time. There is even a statue of him in Budapest. When we were seeking backing it was obvious that the current Lord Rothermere should be the first to be approached.

He was very sympathetic and we found ourselves with the total backing of Associated Newspapers and especially the *Daily Mail*. Instead of meetings with Jaws and the Maxwells we were now meeting regularly with journalists, photographers, PR people and the general managers of newspapers. It was quite a change. Once again a designer was employed, and once again the Barbican Centre was to be submerged in a foreign culture, but this time the rather less known Hungarian culture.

I recall one meeting with particular amusement. A new departmental appointment to manage publicity at the centre had been made and Henry could not have expressed his disapproval more strongly. She was a tall, rangy-looking girl with a heavy north-country accent, piercings and dyed-blond hair. Not his type at all, but she was clever and in time might have made a positive contribution to the centre's work. At the time of this meeting she had only recently joined the staff and none of us knew her well at all.

Henry Wrong chaired the meeting and present were Hans Landesmann, the general manager of the *Daily Mail*, and Vyvyan Harmsworth, who was, among other things, in charge of the newspaper's public relations. Present too, were the head of our arts department; our press officer; one of the arts department managers who was assisting Hans Landesmann; our head of marketing; myself, Colin and a few others. It was a fairly heavyweight group and the discussion was on the subject of the transformation of the centre into something recognisably Hungarian. As there was a certain fear and horror that it might all descend into some sort of gypsy circus, there was a lot of talk of high culture, contemporary Hungarian composers and Hungarian authors. The discussion seemed to go round and round, when the wonderful north-country publicity manager suddenly brought it all down to earth, by saying in her broad accent, 'Well, I don't know about you, but for me it's all goulash and Zsa Zsa Gábor.'

Hungarians suddenly appeared everywhere. There was dear Michael Szell, the gifted fabric designer; Mrs Simpson of Simpsons of Piccadilly, the retail store, who would have tried the patience of a saint; entrepreneurs the de Gelsey brothers, and others who were thrilled by the idea of a Hungarian festival and were anxious to help. One of the most interesting of these was Michael Kovacs, a Hungarian Jew, who had as a small child been taken into a Nazi camp and survived against all the odds. He managed to get to Australia immediately following the war, where he and his wife started out by selling canned fruit. Now he was a very successful gold and jewellery dealer in London and the agent in Britain for Herend porcelain.

I cannot now remember exactly the reasoning behind it, but the *Daily Mail* journalists decided that a visit to Budapest would help them cover the Festival better, and Henry told me that I would be going with them. It was a tremendously interesting time to be visiting Hungary, as the grip of communism on all of Eastern Europe was loosening and Hungary itself was in the process of change. Although we did not know it then, the festival itself would be in the year the Berlin Wall fell. I remember a woman in Budapest telling me that now she could attend Mass quite freely,

A NATION MAKING HISTORY

HUNGARY

At the time of
The Barbican
Magyarok Festival:
a special
Daily Mail review

whereas a few years earlier it would have been unthinkable. It certainly was all very interesting, and I don't think I have ever had such fun; I certainly can't remember laughing more. The party consisted of Vyvyan Harmsworth and his wife Alexandra; Geoffrey Levy, feature writer with the *Daily Mail*, and Ted Blackbrow, the photographer, and myself.

The stops were pulled out and we were treated as very important guests. One of our first meetings was with Ernő Rubik, the professor of architecture who had invented the Rubik cube. From our hotel, we crossed the river and arrived at his very attractive apartment. After waiting some time, an elegantly dressed man, who looked much too young to be a professor of architecture, bounded into the room and proceeded to entertain us. He showed us his next puzzle, which I don't think became much of a success, and, although he wasn't any help with the festival, he was charming and amusing. Of course, we were all given Rubik cubes.

Our next meeting was with Dr Maria Hari, the director of the Pető Institute. Founded by Dr András Pető, the Institute treated children with cerebral palsy or other debilitating diseases with a new method of physical re-education called conductive education, which was considered controversial in some countries, including Britain. Children came to the institute from all over the world, but when we visited it, the majority of foreign children were from the United Kingdom. Their stay in Budapest was lengthy and consequently they were usually accompanied by parents, who simply took up residence there and gave up absolutely everything, including a great deal of money, to have their children treated. Dr Hari was impressive and passionate about the benefits of the treatment. One of its rules seemed to be to let the children have complete freedom. It was all a bit chaotic as children moved about the building as best they could, some walking, some crawling and some rolling about like little sausages. Beyond what I was told and observed that day, I know nothing about conductive education but I did see for myself the hope and faith placed in it by the parents accompanying their disabled children.

There were other working appointments but the final major visit arranged for us was to the Herend porcelain factory, which is a few miles outside Budapest. This visit was really by far the most interesting of all that we saw. The manager of the factory entertained us to lunch in a sort of private canteen; it still felt very much like communism. Our group was seated at a table with a simple white tablecloth, and seated with us were the senior managers of the factory, some of whom spoke a little English. We were served an enormous bowl of very greasy, brownish stew. I looked at it and thought it would be almost impossible to eat. Of course, it would have been very churlish not to show gratitude and enthusiasm when it was so obvious that they were being so hospitable and doing their very best. I ate it.

Halfway through the meal I was surprised to hear the sound of the 'Blue Danube' and other Johann Strauss waltzes being played on a piano, obviously quite nearby. I asked one of our hosts where the music was coming from and he took me into the next room, where, to my utter astonishment, I was greeted by the spectacle of little boys and girls, aged between eight and ten, learning to dance the old-fashioned waltz. Quite unsmiling, the couples were moving slowly across the floor in time to the piano. I was told that these were the children of factory workers who came once a week to learn ballroom dancing. To me it seemed slightly odd in a drab communist country, but none of the Hungarians thought it surprising.

Our tour of the factory was fascinating. We were shown the whole process, but I liked best watching some of the workers painting the almost finished articles. Every single item that comes out of the Herend factory is painted by hand and to see this incredibly delicate and beautiful work being undertaken by the men and women who lived at Herend and who had worked all their lives in the factory was something I will never forget. They showed us examples of Herend work, dinner services for instance, that, for nearly two centuries, had been commissioned by the royal households of Europe. They also showed us a huge, ugly urn commissioned by the Sultan of Brunei. My now friend, Michael Kovacs, was their agent in Britain and I knew that Herend porcelain could be bought only at Fortnum and Mason and a very few other shops in London.

The visit was all over much too soon and we found ourselves back at Heathrow and back at the festival. In a new development, I now found myself totally out of my depth and involved in diplomatic plotting. During all these months of preparation, I had become very friendly with Gábor Földvári, the Hungarian cultural attaché. In Budapest, a political figure of considerable influence, Imre Pozsgay, was causing quite a stir in these dying days of the communist regime and Gábor told me that Pozsgay was planning to visit London. I was told that he would be happy to make an appearance and a speech at a festival reception, if he could meet Mrs Thatcher, who was, of course, then our prime minister. Gábor thought, for some reason, that I was exactly the right person to make these arrangements behind the scenes. 'You must tell no one,' he said. 'But, Gábor, I don't know anybody near Mrs Thatcher and I would not have the slightest idea how to arrange a secret meeting between her and Mr Pozsgay.' 'Well, anyway, will you come and talk to our ambassador about it?' And so, feeling rather foolish, I found myself sitting opposite the Hungarian ambassador in the embassy discussing Gábor's plan. It was all very friendly and polite and we discussed Mr Pozsgay's visit, but I think that the ambassador was as bemused by my presence as I was at being there.

The next thing I knew was that somebody, but not Gábor, contacted Woodrow Wyatt, the Conservative politician and journalist, who was a close friend of Margaret Thatcher and the meeting with Pozsgay was arranged. In his autobiography, Wyatt tells the story in some detail, but does not mention that anyone else was involved. By a happy coincidence, the day before Mrs Thatcher and Mr Pozsgay were to meet, we were holding a reception to launch the festival and Pozsgay agreed to attend and to speak to the guests. We were also told that Mrs Thatcher would come, but only for twenty minutes and that she would not speak and must not be asked to do so. Security was very tight and, as Mrs Thatcher was then the number one target for terrorists in the world, we actually had ex-policemen hidden all over the place, all with guns. There was a small stage with microphones and here Mr Pozsgay was to make his speech. The staff at the embassy had done all they could to smooth the way and support Pozsgay's presence at the festival, while Pozsgay was actively doing all he could to ensure that the communist government, their masters, fell.

It was my job to meet Mrs Thatcher and bring her to the reception. I had not been aware before of quite how small she was, nor how quickly she walked; I was practically running to keep up with her. My other memory is of her incredibly bright blue eyes. We got to the reception and Pozsgay made his speech, through an interpreter. It was a very remarkable speech. Freedom for Eastern Europe really was on the horizon, with Hungary in the vanguard, and he spoke most movingly of the bright future that lay ahead for Hungarians and for all Europeans who had been living under the Russian heel. Mrs Thatcher listened very attentively and the minute he stopped speaking and the applause had died down, she positively snatched the microphone, eyes flashing, and spoke for about twenty minutes. There were probably three hundred people in the room and, this being the arts, I should think that two hundred and fifty of them were anti-Tory; but when she finished one felt that every single one of them would have been willing to die for her. She might have been known as a milk snatcher, but she could be inspiring.

ALL CHANGE

The whole festival was well received. As soon as it was over, plans began for an Israeli festival, which would be held in 1990, again involving the entire centre. The switch from Hungary to Israel was made almost immediately and now, instead of the Hungarian ambassador and his cultural attaché, I found myself dealing with the Israelis. The ambassador was Yoav Biran and I loved him: very clever, attractive and funny, he and his wife became friends of mine and I enjoyed working with him enormously. The cultural attaché was an extraordinary woman, with dyed-red hair and purple lipstick. I remember discussing with her the festival programme brochure, which would have a message from our prime minister and, we hoped, a message from the Israeli president. We knew that it was not quite according to protocol but we were anxious to avoid Israeli party politics and the president seemed a safer bet than any serving politician. Netanyahu was the prime minister and the cultural attaché kept asking me, 'Why not Bibi?' Well, I could not tell her why not Bibi as she might have thought me rude.

I had to visit both the embassy and the ambassador's residence on many occasions and, despite all the experiences I had had, I had never seen such security as I encountered there. The ambassador previous to Yoav Biran had been shot at in the street in London and had been in a vegetative state ever since. The police were very anxious to avoid a repeat. Ambassador Biran was never allowed to be outside the house without protection and this meant, for instance, that he could never decide, on the spur of the moment, to go for a walk. Protection took some time to set up and everything he did had to be pre-arranged. He found it very frustrating.

ISRAEL:
STATE OF THE ART

ISRAEL PHILHARMONIC
ORCHESTRA

Saturday 17 November–
Monday 26 November
1990

BARBICAN CENTRE
Silk Street
London EC2 8DS

On one occasion after a concert we were all going to a reception and he offered me a lift in the embassy car. 'It won't be very comfortable, but you'll never be safer.' I was fascinated. The driver was from the police; sitting next to him was another police officer, and there was one police car in front of us and another immediately behind us. I don't think I've ever seen such driving skill. As we wove through the traffic, the car behind never seemed more than a yard away and remained glued to us until we reached our destination.

While all this was going on, the Barbican plotters had been busy. A weekend meeting was arranged by the Barbican Committee of the Corporation of London, taking place at a country hotel. I was told, but I can't now remember, the exact wording that was to cover the weekend, but it was something like 'The Way Forward for the Barbican Centre'. Present were all the members of the committee and, of course, the director, Henry Wrong. On the Monday morning following the weekend meeting, Henry came into my office in his usual way for the cup of coffee, which Colin as usual made. He looked relaxed and happy and said, 'Well, I really think that the weekend was a success and I am very pleased with the plans and ideas that were discussed.' I expressed my pleasure at hearing this and we chatted for a while, until Henry was told that he was needed to take an urgent telephone call.

He left the office and returned about fifteen minutes later, a completely changed man. His face was chalk white and for the very first time he said, 'Colin, would you mind leaving the office as I want to talk to Moira privately?' After Colin had left he said to me, 'Moira, do you think I should take early retirement?' What had happened was painfully obvious. We talked for perhaps half an hour and the outcome was that Henry saw the best lawyers in London, obtained a very good package, and left the Barbican Centre.

I recognised the inevitability of what had happened and understood a lot of the reasons behind his departure, but I was very sad. Henry Wrong had brought me to the Barbican and had been a kind and supportive boss, very easy to work for. He was a charismatic man with a huge personality and great charm. I believe that it is true to say that without him the Barbican might never have been built and certainly not built within the timescale that it was. I don't think that this has ever been fully acknowledged. In my view, by concentrating on what were essentially trivial matters, the Corporation of London did not appreciate the immensity of his contribution to the Barbican Centre. Richard York, his deputy, was to be in charge of our affairs until a new appointment was made and one day soon afterwards, he told me that I would have to leave my job at the end of December as I would be turning sixty-five in January. This was the rule of the Corporation. I understood that he would do nothing to interfere with this process and that I would have to leave. I also knew that if Henry had still been the director, he would have found a way round the rules and probably employed me as a consultant, but he was not the director and so, very sadly, I prepared to quit at the end of December.

The process needed to find my replacement was started immediately. I gathered that there were several applicants and, at the end of two rounds of interviews, Richard York came into my office and said that, after seeing everyone, they had been left with two candidates and were finding it hard to come to a final decision. 'Would you mind seeing them and letting us know what you think?' I duly interviewed both the candidates and said to Richard, 'I really can't recommend either of them, but I can tell you that Colin would do the job much better than either of them.' 'Colin! He's far too young.' 'Nevertheless, Richard, I am telling you that he would be by far the best candidate.' And so Colin was interviewed, asked to produce a presentation and finally appointed the head of development. I was delighted and subsequently Colin has had a stunningly successful career. His time at the Barbican was a success, and from there he went on to do ten years as head of development at the National Gallery, five years as the director of the Charleston Trust, and is now the director of the House of Illustration.

While I was getting used to the idea of leaving my job, still quite upset about no one ever mentioning this age rule to me at the outset, and wondering what I would do next, Clive Gillinson, managing director of the London Symphony Orchestra, asked me to have lunch with him. As the LSO was one of the tenant companies in the Barbican and we had worked closely with the orchestra when presenting international festivals, I knew Clive well. Now, having been made very aware of my age, I was totally unprepared when, over lunch, he offered me the job of head of development for the LSO. I felt flattered, of course, but anxious and I said, 'But Clive, I am going to be sixty-five next month.' 'I am not at all interested in your age and I think that you can do the job.' And so began one of the best periods of my life.

I was terribly excited by the prospect of another new chapter opening and was looking forward to a new challenge. I was also looking forward to working for the most prestigious orchestra in the United Kingdom. I knew that Clive Gillinson was a tremendously successful general manager and I was looking forward to working for him. I decided to take the opportunity to have a holiday before I started my new job and I went to Australia to see my son, David.

Working for an orchestra was unlike anything I had done before. Both Aldeburgh and the Barbican were multi-faceted and there were so many different aspects to sponsorship, to what needed money most and what we could offer the sponsors. With the orchestra, sponsorship was entirely focused and, in that respect, easier.

The LSO administration consisted of about eighteen people and we were rather crowded in our Barbican Centre offices. In one sense, it was like being back in Aldeburgh; a small staff of very bright, intelligent young people who worked very hard and at the same time had a tremendous amount of fun. There was a lot of laughter. Clive was a brilliant boss and I learned an enormous amount from him. He micro-managed everything; with anyone else, I think I would have found it extremely irritating but it became for me just the way Clive worked and that made it all right.

As well as the administration, there was the orchestra and, of course, I got to know all its members. The LSO has always had the reputation of being feisty, to say the least, but I found them supportive of my efforts and I made some very good friends. Clive expected 100 per cent commitment from his staff and this meant that we were expected to attend concerts, which far from being a duty was a luxury. Usually there were two concerts a week and this meant that I listened to an extraordinary amount of wonderful music.

I also got to know the conductors. Slava Rostropovich conducted the LSO frequently and it was nice once again to find myself in one of his bear hugs, kissed over and over and called Moirushka. Galina came to his concerts and it was a delight to see her too, but I did not have the close relationship that I had had with her in Aldeburgh; I think she felt that the LSO was very much Slava's territory, whereas at Aldeburgh she had been directly involved. I got to know Colin Davis, that remarkable musician, and the elegant Michael Tilson Thomas, who wore the best-fitting tails that I have ever seen. As at Aldeburgh, one got entirely used to seeing the most famous musicians in the world having a cup of coffee in the office.

Raising sponsorship, although focused, was taxing and it was hard work. This was the height of Japanese ascendancy in the financial world. The Japanese at one time were our main sponsors. This was due mainly to Mr Yamataka. Yamasan, as I learned to call him, was a small, bald Japanese banker with huge ambitions to become part of the British establishment. He had got to know Clive and offered to help the LSO with Japanese sponsorship, and his help was invaluable. In return he was given the title of 'International Vice President', a title invented by Clive. He had excellent contacts and when we had to go to meetings, he would guide me. He taught me about the etiquette of making a pitch to a Japanese VIP and how to avoid the pitfalls that, I'm sure, would otherwise have followed quite naturally.

A couple of years later the LSO was to tour Japan and it was decided that the Emperor and Empress should be invited to one of the concerts. I had to compose a letter to the chamberlain and I struggled to word it, knowing that it had to be simultaneouly flattering and grovelling. After several attempts I produced something nauseating, which I hoped would express sufficient grovelling. I sent it to Yamasan for vetting and I was dismayed when he telephoned and said, 'No good. Not flowery enough.' Well, what was I to do? I didn't know how to be more flowery. So it was back to the drawing board and I suppose what I eventually did was considered all right because, to everyone's delight, the Emperor and Empress set a precedent by accepting the invitation.

Yamasan could be very touchy; working with him was a minefield. There were several occasions when I somehow managed to offend him and both an apology (more grovelling) and sending flowers was the only way out of it. Once we had the Japanese ambassador due to attend a concert and I, thinking that I was doing my job, went down to the Barbican's roadside to meet him. Apparently I should not have done this and Yamasan was white with fury as he told me, 'You have taken away my face.'

Part of his ambition to become an English gentleman now reached fruition. 'Moira,' he said, 'I have very good news to tell you.' What was the good news, I asked, and he said, 'I am now a member of a club, a gentleman's club.' Given our fairly recent history I was somewhat surprised when, answering my question as to which one, he said, 'The Naval and Military Club.'

On another occasion, Yamasan, Clive and I were to meet for lunch following Yamasan's holiday, which had included a visit to Hawaii. In *Fawlty Towers* style we told each other not to mention Pearl Harbor, but, to our amazement, he was the one who talked about it. Truly it is difficult for us to understand the Japanese mind and without his help I could not possibly have achieved such a high level of Japanese sponsorship. I suppose it was just a part of the puzzling picture when both his clever daughters went to St Andrews to read theology.

The orchestra toured an awful lot and although it was not my job to go with them I did go on tour on three occasions. The first time was to New York and then I went twice to Israel.

Clive told me that he had been approached with a proposal to take the orchestra to Israel following the end of the First Gulf War, when no foreign orchestra felt able to go and, of course, when there were no tourists. This was, after all, the war when rockets were fired on Tel Aviv and everybody was still understandably nervous. Clive asked me what I thought. It would mean raising sufficient funds to pay for everything as nobody in Israel could afford to support us. The costs were high but we decided to try and as one person replied when I asked for his support, 'Israel and music – how can I refuse?'

I said, half jokingly, that a condition of getting the money was that I would be allowed to go too, and so I found myself on a flight with all the band, Michael Tilson Thomas our conductor; Joshua Robeson, Michael's manager, and Maxim Vengarov, our soloist. Also travelling with us were Michael and Dvora Lewis, Henry Wrong (I can't now remember why he was there), and a supporter of the orchestra, Amina Harris. Dvora was the LSO's PR and press representative and was without any doubt the most highly regarded in her field; she and her husband Michael had become great friends of mine and are still to this day important in my life. Amina Harris is an Israeli with a British father and an Israeli mother and her parents were the most generous and kindly people.

We stayed in Tel Aviv but apart from the concerts there, we had one concert in Jerusalem and one in Haifa. On the day of the Jerusalem concert I was told that I could get a lift on the coach and spend the day in Jerusalem. It is probably one of the most amazing days of my life, one that I will certainly never forget. As we drove through the outskirts and into the city, the driver would suddenly say, 'There's the Mount of Olives' or 'There's the Garden of Gethsemane', and I wanted to yell out and tell him to stop. Rushing past at speed, I just couldn't take it all in.

There were absolutely no tourists to be seen and Jerusalem seemed deserted. A little group of five of us made our way to the Church of the Holy Sepulchre and I saw for the first time the tiny winding streets, as narrow as footpaths, with shop owners sitting in their doorways, disconsolate because of the lack of tourists, trying to sell their wares. I actually felt almost frightened as we wound our way through this labyrinth of streets, realising how very easy it would be to get lost. Finally we reached the Holy Sepulchre and, apart from the Russian Orthodox priests, there was not another person there. Having seen on television the sort of crowds that normally throng the church, packed like sardines, and surely unable to see anything, I knew how incredibly fortunate we were. It was actually possible to look at everything, take one's time and think.

I loved Tel Aviv, despite the noise, the bustling, brash people, impossibly rude taxi drivers and all the rest of it; I just loved being there. One evening three of us walked along the beach to Jaffa to have dinner and the walk beside the sea on that balmy evening is one of the memories I treasure. I still have a picture in my mind of the fruit and vegetable markets and all the incredible colours everywhere.

The concerts were all sold out and the Israeli concertgoers expressed their gratitude to us. In the absence of any other foreign orchestra, they thought we were very brave. The programme consisted of Britten's *The Young Person's Guide to the Orchestra* and the Beethoven Violin Concerto, with Michael Tilson Thomas conducting and Maxim Vengarov as soloist. I can never hear either of these pieces now without thinking that I am back in Tel Aviv.

The orchestra returned to Israel again in 1998 to join in the celebrations for the fiftieth anniversary year of the founding of the state of Israel. Again I was lucky enough to go with them, this time because some concerts in the tour had been sponsored by Land Rover and some by Sema Group who were long-time supporters of the LSO. The sponsors had arranged to entertain guests at the concerts and it was my job to look after them. The

Land Rover sponsorship had been very complicated and very difficult; it was worth a lot of money and I felt that we had earned every penny because of the demanding and fault-finding people I had been dealing with. The sponsorship consultant they employed was actually a friend of mine, but she certainly knew how to get her pound of flesh. I rather admired her.

I cannot express how happy I was to be working for the LSO. Yes, it was very pressured and often stressful and we all worked very hard, but I don't think I have ever had so much fun. And not only fun. For me personally it was a time of development. I was learning all the time and not just about my job. There was the inestimable privilege of listening to world-class music, meeting fascinating people and generally broadening my experience. But during my career with the LSO, there was a break of just over two years.

RETURN TO ZIMBABWE

In 1993 I remarried. My new husband was a very old friend, a widower, who lived in Zimbabwe. His wife had also been a very good friend of mine. As he had been educated in England, both at school and at Oxford and as two of his three children were living in England, I expected him to want to live here and, indeed, he himself expressed this wish. We agreed that we would, at the beginning, divide our time between the two countries and I privately thought that I would be able to change that to, perhaps, three months there and the rest of the year here. I married thinking that with an old friend I would enjoy happy companionship and, I have to admit, a degree of security that at the time was rather lacking in my life.

I was very foolish and I discovered on my return that the new independent Zimbabwe was really rather more awful than Rhodesia had been. The first difference and one of the horrors that made it worse was the epidemic of Aids. The young, male population was dying in vast numbers, leaving grieving families and hundreds of thousands of orphans; the lucky ones were cared for by grandmothers but the unlucky ones had nowhere to go. I visited a tea plantation near what used to be called Umtali. The owner of the plantation told me that he did not know how long he could carry on. Tea is a very labour-intensive crop and he told me that he was losing members of his work force on a daily basis.

Added to this, as far as I was concerned, was the fact that Harare (formerly Salisbury) had become a very dangerous place. There was an appalling amount of unemployment and desperate people were quick to turn to crime in order to live. I was told that when I was driving a car, I should always be conscious that there might be someone following me. If I suspected that was what was happening, I should not go home and turn into our own drive as I would be attacked when I got out of the car. I should never drive with the window down. Houses were surrounded by high walls or high fences with razor wire on top of them and gates were locked. Robert Mugabe was the president and he was even better at promoting himself than Ian Smith had been. He lived in what had previously been the residence of the governor general (with a lot of additions) and after 6 p.m. no one was allowed to drive on the roads that lay alongside his property. While I was there the son of a former governor of the Bank of England, Robin Leigh-Pemberton, possibly after enjoying an evening with friends, drove along one of these roads by mistake and died after the car was shot at by Mugabe's guards.

Household shopping was difficult. There were some shops that sold luxury goods but supplies of ordinary things such as lavatory paper were unreliable; one week the shops would be full and then for the following three weeks everything would have disappeared. But none of this was as bad as the boredom. There was an unreadable daily newspaper; the television news, read by regime-approved presenters, was unwatchable, and all the rest of the television output consisted of old, third-rate American sitcoms. I found the perpetual presence of servants in the house very oppressive; there was absolutely no privacy, no escape from eyes that were always watching, observing.

The black–white divide was, in many ways, as it had always been. It is true that there was a black government and there were no longer separate queues in the post offices, but the white population was still prosperous and there was terrible poverty in the black townships and in the rural areas.

Each time I was back in England, I faced the return to Zimbabwe with increasing dread. My husband, far from wanting to live in England, as I had expected, felt exactly the reverse and seemed to loathe the time we spent here. It was an impossible situation and, at my age, it seemed stupid to waste valuable time trying to rescue something that I thought could probably not be rescued. It was all a humiliating experience and a terrible mistake but I decided to cut my losses and come back home alone.

I was incredibly fortunate. During the time that I was away, I had never felt far from the LSO and when I returned I was soon in touch with Clive. Someone had been doing my job but, I gathered, not been an unqualified success. To my utter delight, I was offered my old job. I think that Clive was as pleased as I was and I found myself back in the familiar routine among familiar faces. It was as though I had never been away and many of the experiences I have written about here, such as the Israeli tours, took place after my return.

During all the time I worked for the LSO, the most important project in which I was involved was the conversion of St Luke's. Our education programme was just developing and Clive thought that it would need its own dedicated home. At the same time he was anxious to find an extra rehearsal space for the orchestra. He gave Emma Chesters, the Head of Education at the time, the task of finding a suitable building and she came back with details of St Luke's, a redundant Hawksmoor church in Old Street, very convenient for the Barbican.

The church was roofless and in ruins with long grass growing in the nave but the architecture was superb and the magnificent steeple was still standing. The cost of conversion was enormous and we were presented with the daunting prospect of raising millions. We managed to come to a pro-bono arrangement with KPMG who undertook all the complicated accountancy work and with Clifford Chance for all the legal work. This was a tremendous help. We applied for financial support from both the Arts and Heritage funds of the Lottery, and we applied to all the major trusts, including the Bridge House Trust, all of whom saw the value of the project and responded with great generosity. Levitt Bernstein were chosen as the architects and they produced plans for a beautiful conversion, undertaken with sensitivity and understanding of our aims.

The major sponsor was UBS, a Swiss global financial services company, to whom we offered naming rights in return for what was then the most expensive arts sponsorship in the country. This involved very complicated negotiations not exactly helped by what became known as the key fiasco. The UBS managers in London said that their senior directors in Zurich would be visiting London and wanted to inspect the site and the actual church building. At the time the church was still the property of the Diocese of London and I arranged for their keeper of the keys to meet us at St Luke's on a certain date at 8 a.m. as the Swiss wanted to make an early start.

We were all in place – Clive, Dvora Lewis, our PR consultant, myself and the key keeper – when two large black cars arrived with the Swiss directors. The man with the keys then went to unlock the huge lock on the gate, which was the only entrance to the church grounds, and when I saw that he was having a considerable struggle I realised that he had the wrong keys. I was both embarrassed and angry and I went up to him at the gate and hissed, 'This is extremely embarrassing', horribly aware of our potential sponsors standing around and beginning to look tetchy. 'It's even more embarrassing for me' was his rather unsatisfactory reply. However, he showed great initiative, went away to where there were some building works and came back with a hacksaw, with which he proceeded to attack the lock and break in. I was slightly nervous that the police might appear at any moment.

Despite such a spectacular setback and many other difficulties, including discovering that the crypt was a plague burial ground, the sponsorship was successfully negotiated. We had help and encouragement from Lisa Spiro, my friend Diney's daughter, who worked for UBS and was concerned with their social responsibility scheme. Eventually, after what seemed like an endless series of meetings and an endless series of crises, the conversion was complete and St Luke's stands today, saved from demolition, a truly beautiful building, the home of the LSO's Discovery programme and a landmark in that part of London.

BACK AT THE BARBICAN

My life continued to be happy and fulfilling and was to continue to be so for the next three years. The only real changes that occurred were changes of personnel and some of these changes took place in my own department. I suppose that one must always be prepared for rotten apples. I had encountered one when I was at Aldeburgh and now, in my department, there was another. It takes only one person to have a malign influence and everything is affected and then, in my experience, everyone becomes unhappy. This one particular person in the department was a trouble-maker. She made an ally of a very junior member of the department and there was an awful lot of giggling and the exchange of mischief-making

top The London Symphony Orchestra in the Barbican Hall
bottom left Clive Gillinson, General Manager of the LSO
bottom right With Rostropovich at an LSO party

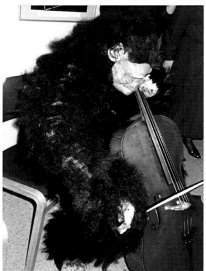

top Mstislav Rostropovich conducting the LSO
bottom left Rostropovich in a gorilla costume . . .
bottom right . . . and enjoying the bath in his London home

Principal Conductors of the LSO:
Sir Colin Davis (*top*) and Michael Tilson Thomas (*below*)

top left Being presented to Her Majesty The Queen after
an LSO concert at the Barbican Centre
top right With HRH The Prince of Wales and Sarah Derbyshire
before a Live Music Now concert at Windsor Castle
bottom St Luke's, the LSO Education Centre

emails. At the same time, we had a tragic situation to deal with, too. The wife of a very nice young man in the department gave birth to a seriously disabled baby and, naturally, he wanted to spend as much time as possible at the hospital. This meant extra work for the others and my two trouble-makers really did make trouble, refusing to help and refusing to take on some of the extra work the young man's absence caused. When I think of it I still feel guilty and I hope he has forgiven me. I certainly did not support him as vigorously as I should have; the trouble-maker left not long afterwards which was a very good thing.

I loved the LSO but all the unhappiness that was being caused at this particular time and the knowledge that I was getting older made me decide, after a while, that I should leave and that a younger person should take over my work. I was absolutely miserable about leaving. The fact that the players at the orchestra's AGM gave me a standing ovation in recognition of my work when it was announced that I was leaving, and the wonderful farewell party given by the administration somehow only made me unhappier. It was as though I was leaving my family and for a long while I felt bereft.

When I first went to work for the Barbican, I had bought a flat in Clapham and, although it was a very nice flat, I started to hate it. Apart from the journey backwards and forwards in rush-hour traffic, if I had been to a concert and a reception afterwards, it was often very late when I set out for home. This meant that finding a parking place near the flat was difficult and often I had to leave the car some distance away. This was followed by a walk to the flat and I found it very frightening; I had to turn a corner where a large shrub overhung the pavement and as I went round that corner, my heart used to beat very fast indeed. I can still remember clearly my fear walking along those streets after midnight.

Sometime before I left the LSO, I had decided to sell my flat and rent in the Barbican. The Board of the LSO was extremely kind to me, because unless you could find a flat to rent privately (and I could not) the only way to do this was to rent from the Corporation of London itself, who were, of course, the owners. They would rent only to registered companies and, in order to solve the problem, the LSO very kindly agreed to become the official lessees. I moved into Willoughby House, which I absolutely loved. My walk to the office took me five minutes. I had a parking place and there was a twenty-four-hour, seven-days-a-week parking attendant. I was very happy.

It was while living in the Barbican, where I felt so safe and so happy, that, ironically, I was mugged. It was during the Christmas period and I had been to a concert at the Barbican, but I decided to leave after the interval. I think it was one of those horrible Christmas concerts. Before I left, I was joking with some of the backstage boys, whom I knew quite well, and then got into the lift to get to my level and go back to the flat. Of course, as the concert was still happening, there was no one around and I was walking alone in semi-darkness, but I was not afraid at all. I knew every bit of this building well and, as far as I was concerned, there was nothing to be afraid of. Suddenly someone behind me grabbed me round the waist and held me terribly tightly. For just a moment, I thought that it was one of the backstage boys fooling around, but I soon realised that it was not. I was holding my handbag very loosely and if that was what he wanted, there was nothing to stop him taking it. But he didn't. He just continued to hold me very tightly.

By a stroke of incredibly good fortune, the night boilerman was coming round the corner to go to his work. He rushed up to me to help and my attacker fled. If he had run out of the building, he would have got away but Darren Malone (his name, I later discovered) was not very clever, and ran *into* the building, ending up in one of the lavatories, where the police found him. Two City of London policemen escorted me home and although I was shaken, I was quite unhurt.

Soon after I got home the concert ended. News of the attack reached the players and one by one they appeared at my flat to make sure that I was all right. There were also some members of the administration there. I almost began to laugh. It was getting exactly like the ship's cabin in the Marx Brothers film, *A Night at the Opera*, as more and more people squashed into the flat. I was very touched by their concern. Then the police arrived to take a statement from me. I told a female officer what had had happened and she took notes, which she then read back to me. It sounded exactly like Ernie Wise and 'the play what I wrote'. I thought of making corrections, as the statement would be read out in court as my words, but I decided I couldn't be bothered. Even though I sounded like Ernie Wise, Darren Malone was ordered to pay me £100, for which I am still waiting.

The next morning as I was preparing to work, I was telephoned by a representative of Victim Support, who wanted to come and see me. I had enormous difficulty in persuading her that there was really no need and that I just wanted to go to the office. She was very persistent and when I absolutely refused to be counselled, I could hear the disappointment in her voice. Poor woman, at last an opportunity to put into practice all those training sessions, only to have the offer of support refused.

Despite this, I really liked living in the Barbican, but there was a worry. I had no home of my own and I knew that if I were not working I would not be able to afford the Barbican rent. I decided that I had to buy somewhere but was not at all certain where that place should be. Should I stay in London? Probably too expensive. Should I go back to Suffolk? This idea was knocked on the head when, during a weekend visit to friends, I found myself walking down the Thoroughfare in Woodbridge; coming towards me there was nothing except Barbour jackets, green wellies and those loud braying voices. I knew without doubt that it was not the place for me. In the end I settled on Brighton, raffish and sleazy, near enough London and in those days not too expensive. I bought a flat in Hove, but on the Brighton–Hove border, not deepest Hove which I would not have liked.

BRIGHTON, AND DEFINITELY NOT RETIRING

When I first left the LSO and went to live in Brighton, I thought that I had made a dreadful mistake and I didn't like it at all. I was lonely and I used often to think, 'What on earth am I doing in this horrible place?' It took longer than I thought to change that feeling but I started to make friends and gradually to make a life for myself. In time I changed my mind completely and I decided that I had actually made a good move.

One of the reasons for my change of heart was that in 1997 I was received into the Catholic Church and found myself with friends and something very like a family. I had been obsessed with the Church as a child and as an adult I had always had Catholic leanings, but remembering my father's antagonism to Catholicism and everything about it, I had always felt that if I did anything about it, I would, in some way, be betraying him. I had loved him much too much to do that. The consequence was that, absurdly, I had to reach the age of seventy-two before I freed myself of this inhibition. Becoming a Catholic has been the most important and by far the best decision of my life: I had come home.

Immediately after leaving the LSO I found myself working on a part-time basis for Masterprize, a competition for composers established by my friend and colleague John McLaren to encourage audiences to be more interested in new music. John is an extraordinary person who started his professional life in the Foreign Office, then changed career, and went into banking. There is nothing very strange about that, but he, at the same time, became a successful novelist; eventually he had seven or eight titles to his name. He initiated and oversaw Masterprize, which was a huge undertaking. He threw his heart and soul (and his money) completely into the project, which saw three events in London, attracting worldwide attention. Masterprize cemented my friendship with John; it remains a highly valued and important friendship to this day.

The competition was open to composers of classical music who were invited to submit scores to a panel of judges and from these initial submissions a certain number were selected to go forward to the next stage. The final selections were broadcast in all European Union countries and the votes of these radio audiences counted towards the final selection. The finalists had their work performed by the London Symphony Orchestra at a concert at the Barbican, where there was an audience vote and a panel of judges to choose a winner. The prize money was substantial and a considerable draw, especially for young, unknown composers.

It was a brilliant idea that should have captured the imagination of all the vast numbers of people who enjoy listening to classical music, but there were flaws in the structure, which, I think, became apparent only later. For one thing, established composers did not enter as they felt that they could not be seen to fail. With a radio audience and a live audience in the concert hall able to wield such a major influence, the finalists' work tended to be rather banal and much of it sounded a bit like film music. It was a huge exercise and it was undoubtedly a success in that it did bring new music to the attention of a very large audience.

John asked me to join the team during the planning stage and to help with fundraising. I thoroughly enjoyed my association with Masterprize and enjoyed working for John. There was tremendous enthusiasm for the project and we were all fired up with this spirit. John also employed a fundraiser in New York, one of those humourless Americans who spoke very deliberately and very slowly. She was constantly telling us that she had to get all her ducks in a row. Ducks in a row or not, she was not a great success and confirmed my opinion that, in general, Americans just do not fit when fundraising for a British project.

For the first two or three years after leaving the LSO, as well as working for Masterprize, I did a certain amount of freelance consultancy. On the whole I don't have a very high opinion of consultants and I never expected to find myself among their ranks, but I was lucky and I was offered really interesting work. One job was with the Orchestra of the Age of Enlightenment and this was thoroughly enjoyable, mainly because of the personnel involved. David Pickard was the director of the OAE (subsequently of Glyndebourne and the BBC Proms) and Kirsty MacDonald was their development manager – two very nice people to work with. I also did a fundraising feasibility study for a capital appeal to be undertaken by the Hampstead Theatre, which I am glad to say turned out to be very successful.

It was at this time that we had a great family celebration. My father-in-law, F. S. Bennett, who had been a pioneer of the motor industry, imported the first Cadillac into the United Kingdom in 1903. Shortly after the car's arrival, he undertook the RAC Run, driving the car for five consecutive days, each journey starting in London and ending in a town in the South East – each a distance of fifty miles from London. In 1953, by now into his eighties, he repeated this feat in the same car, with Stirling Moss as his driving partner. After his death in 1958 the car was placed on permanent loan in the Beaulieu Museum, where it is well looked after. In 2003, exactly a hundred years after his grandfather's achievement, Julian undertook the same challenge in the same old car. It was very difficult, not least because a car designed for 1903 conditions was not exactly prepared for the traffic on the roads of 2003, but he did it and made us all very proud. I was there when he drove to Brighton where he was given a civic welcome, with people cheering him on.

One day, completely out of the blue, I was contacted by Ian Stoutzker, whom I had known for a long time as he was the chairman of the LSO Advisory Council. Ian was responsible for an organisation called Live Music Now, which had been founded by Yehudi Menuhin with Ian's support and help. It is a wonderful organisation and had grown out of an idea that Menuhin had when visiting the concentration camps after the end of the Second World War. He played to some of the survivors, with

Benjamin Britten as his accompanist, and, realising how important and how healing live music can be, he decided to found an organisation in the United Kingdom that would bring live music of the very highest standard to people who otherwise would not have access to it. And that is how the idea was born.

Young postgraduate musicians, up to the age of twenty-seven, would be selected through a rigorous audition process and then paid proper professional fees to take live music into prisons, day centres, homes for disabled children, schools that had no such opportunities for their pupils – in fact anywhere where such an experience would be new. It really was a win–win situation. The venues paid nothing as Live Music Now raised the money to pay the musicians and all associated costs, and people who often had little access to music experienced the joy of live performance. An added bonus was that the young musicians had to learn presentation skills and this was a considerable help in their future careers.

Ian asked me whether I would take over the fundraising and although he and I had not always seen eye to eye, I was happy to take it on, particularly after I met Sarah Derbyshire, who was the director. She and I did see eye to eye and for the three years that I worked for Live Music Now we both enjoyed working together and we always managed to find something to laugh about. After particularly difficult meetings of all the governors in Ian's Belgravia house, we would often stagger out into the street and head straight for the Berkeley and a glass of champagne.

Live Music Now is a nationwide organisation and has branches through-out the United Kingdom. Each branch has a director responsible for the fundraising for that particular branch and my job was to raise money for the central administrative costs, including such things as the regional directors' salaries. I thought that this was a very bad structure and I did my best to get it changed. I was unsuccessful and, perhaps as a result, Ian had begun to treat me with considerable suspicion and often downright hostility. I have never understood why he behaved as he did. Quite often and very bewilderingly, he would suddenly adopt a completely different attitude, all kisses and hugs and lunch at an expensive restaurant. The fundraising was a success and I managed to persuade two wonderful former colleagues of mine to apply to become directors when vacancies occurred. One of these was Trudy White, who became the London branch director and the other was Karen Irwin, who was director of the North

East branch and had formerly been head of education at the LSO. I felt by suggesting these two outstanding people join Live Music Now, I had made a significant contribution to the organisation but I don't think that Ian Stoutzker would have agreed.

I was working for Live Music Now when the London bombings occurred on 7 July 2005. We were holding auditions that day at the Royal Academy of Music in Marylebone Road and although I frequently attended the auditions, on this occasion I had arranged to stay in the office. Our office was on the top floor of an old building in Lower Belgrave Street, owned by the Grosvenor Estate, and let to us for a very low rental because it was in such a bad state of repair; it leaked like a sieve. The stairs were especially hazardous and creaked ominously with every step. The only other tenant at the top of the building was the New London Orchestra, managed by Julian Knight.

That day I got into my office shortly after 9 o'clock and found that the entire building was empty except for Julian working next door. There was no one else in his office and no one else in mine. At about ten o'clock he came into my office saying, 'Moira, there are bombs going off all over London.' We watched the news on our computers with mounting horror. All the tube stations and railway stations were shut, there were no buses, and I had no idea how I would get home. Julian left at about noon and I was quite alone, a bit frightened and very worried. My son Julian and his wife Polly telephoned several times, trying to make arrangements for me to stay in London – somewhere I could reach – but they were unsuccessful. All the streets around Victoria station were closed off, and from my office window I could look directly on to Buckingham Palace Road, which was heaving with people, all looking lost and bewildered and obviously with no idea how to get anywhere. As it was summer, there were a lot of tourists, and I watched them, dragging suitcases up and down Buckingham Palace Road, quite clearly not knowing what to do, and nobody there to tell them. Although there were policemen everywhere, they didn't know what was going to happen either, and were not much comfort to the tourists or to anybody else.

I spoke to Sarah Derbyshire at the Royal Academy, and I was told that two of the young musicians had arrived with blackened faces, having been rather too near where the bombs had exploded. Every single one of those expected for auditions got there, which was amazing; they all showed courage and initiative. Of course, I was still in the office but at about 4 p.m. some of the streets were opened and I thought that Victoria station might open too, but knowing what the crowds would be like on the trains, I sat where I was until I thought it might be possible to travel. Eventually I left the office and literally squeezed myself on to a train leaving for Brighton. It was very slow and stopped a lot, but eventually I arrived home, after a dreadful day, horrified by the loss of life and by the pictures of distraught people searching frantically for members of their families. Terrorism had certainly come to London.

My career with Live Music Now culminated with a concert and reception to be held at Windsor Castle. Ian Stoutzker was very friendly with Michael Fawcett, who had been a valet to the Prince of Wales and had now become his right-hand man. Before the event, I went to the castle with Ian to do a sort of recce and to meet Michael Fawcett, who was dressed in a very smart blazer, gold cufflinks in evidence; he had clearly put the days of being a valet a long way behind him. From the outset, I was deeply suspicious of him, particularly so when he announced that he could arrange for a friend of his to be responsible for the design and production of the programmes and menus. I would have said no if it had been my decision but Ian found his ideas irresistible. How right I was to be suspicious. The programmes were vulgar, with dreadful maroon ribbons everywhere, and they were also frightfully expensive. But it seemed that Michael Fawcett could do no wrong. However, the concert itself was very good. Matthew Wadsworth, the blind lutenist, performed most beautifully and the dinner afterwards went well, despite the awful programmes and the hideous menus. After this I found Ian's unpredictability just too much and I decided that I had had enough. He had probably had enough too.

IRISH CONNECTIONS

My friend and colleague John Owen had for some time had close connections with Ireland. Some years earlier he and I were invited to the wedding in Belfast of one of the musicians who had studied at Aldeburgh and with whom we, and especially John, had maintained close contact. Una Hunt was the musician. Her father treated us with extraordinary generosity, paying for guests from England to stay at the rather glamorous country-house hotel where the wedding reception would be held. This was at the height of the Troubles and although it was a Catholic wedding there was a completely mixed crowd invited. I remember remarking on this to a young man who came from Belfast and he said, 'He must have paid the Boys.' Whether he paid them or not, we all had a lovely time.

John and I had decided to spend a few more days in Ireland and we hired a car to drive down to Dublin. On the journey south we reached Newry, not far from the border with the Republic of Ireland, and decided to stop for lunch and to buy a CD to play in the car. We wandered about until we found a music shop. Although there were a number of British soldiers in the town, we felt that we might have been in any small, rather dull town in the United Kingdom. After my return when I told friends about this, they were aghast. 'What, you stopped in Newry? Didn't you know that it is one of the most dangerous places in Northern Ireland?'

One day on that visit to Dublin, we decided to drive into the countryside and have a picnic, so we stopped in a village to buy provisions. There was a pub nearby. A drink seemed an attractive idea and we found ourselves inside this very dark pub where it seemed no light ever penetrated. We stuck out like sore thumbs – our voices were wrong and our car had a Belfast number plate. I don't think I have ever experienced such hostility. Not a word was said but the looks from the old biddies who sat, lining the walls, were such that we decided to leave at once, not bothering to finish our drinks.

John had established close links in the Irish Republic and, in fact, bought a piece of land in County Clare, where he was later to build a beautiful house. At the time he was working for the Irish Chamber Orchestra and he asked me to meet John Kelly, who was the general manager of the ICO, which was resident at Limerick University. I did, and John Kelly suggested that I might undertake some work for him. This was to prove interesting and very enjoyable. (This was now after the Good Friday Agreement.)

John Kelly is a rather flamboyant person, a violinist himself, he seemed to take complete ownership of the orchestra and his views were often at odds with others, including those of the board of trustees. He was immensely ambitious for the orchestra, wanting it, he said, to be the 'Berlin Philharmonic' of chamber orchestras. He had great imagination and vision and however much people might have sniggered behind his back, laughing at what they saw as his vanity, one could not but be impressed. John believed that God would ensure that all his dreams and visions for the ICO, or anything else for that matter, would become reality. He wanted the orchestra to have its own premises on the university campus and I was amazed when, against all the odds, the beautiful ICO building was opened. The rehearsal space was described by a French conductor as one of the best in Europe. This is but one example of the Almighty apparently intervening to bring to life one of John's rather lofty ideas.

John was kind and supportive to me. Nick Winter, a colleague from Aldeburgh, was the general manager of the ICO, so I felt I was among friends. An additional plus was that John Owen's house had now been built and I stayed with him on many occasions. It really was a wonderful house, designed by John himself, with curved walls and a wonderful curving staircase. Outside it looked rather like any small, rural Irish house, with white walls, but once the front door was opened you found yourself transported into a minimalist structure that would not have looked out of place in Manhattan.

Usually when I was working for the ICO I stayed in a hotel in Kilaloe, a lovely little town on Lake Dergh. The hotel was attractive and staffed by Poles and Lithuanians, which seemed to be the norm in Ireland. They didn't speak much English. Nick Winter had a house near the hotel and we often had dinner together, which was an added bonus as he and I had known each other for such a long time. It was a particular pleasure for me as only a couple of years earlier Nick had been left for dead after being attacked while walking in Siberia. He speaks Russian fluently, as well as several other languages, and his great joy in life is undertaking very long, solitary wilderness walks. It was while doing one of these that he had been mugged and very severely injured, but fortunately he managed to drag himself to a dwelling nearby and throw stones at the windows to attract attention. A teacher lived there and called the local doctor, who had served in the Russian forces where he had seen terrible injuries and was used to operating in primitive conditions. Had this not been so, it is unlikely that he would have been brave enough to perform a very complicated procedure on Nick, more or less on the kitchen table. In doing so he undoubtedly saved Nick's life before a surgeon – urgently summoned – arrived to complete the operation.

I enjoyed my Irish job. The members of the orchestra were fun and there was a very warm spirit of camaraderie. They made me feel welcome and very much a member of the organisation. Part of the brief was that I help them find someone to take charge of their sponsorship department and I recommended a young man I knew in London, someone I thought would do the job well. He was duly appointed and, to my astonishment and utter dismay, proved to be an absolute disaster. It was a very humbling experience. Although it was true that my candidate never managed to concentrate fully on the job and did not really like being in Ireland, I became certain that, to be successful, the person appointed would have to be Irish. Everyone was friendly and we all worked together well, but we were in Ireland, and underneath I felt that there would always be a 'them and us' tension. In the often delicate business of attracting sponsors I believed that being 'one of us' would help.

Apart from my colleagues in the administration and the players in the orchestra there were interesting people on their board of directors. I liked them and got to know some of them well. One woman, whose home was not far from Limerick, was the first woman to have been called to the Bar in London and she had an endless fund of fascinating tales. I met Irish composers and Irish poets as well as Irish bankers and the chief executives of Irish companies. The poets and composers all insisted on their names being expressed in Irish and they were completely incomprehensible to me. Despite inter-governmental agreements, I realised feelings still ran high, which, I suppose, was understandable.

I am aware that I was fortunate and I am certainly grateful for the time I spent in Limerick and the friendships I made, but despite its beauty and the kindness shown to me by individuals, I never felt entirely comfortable in Ireland. There was something brooding and dark that seemed to hang over everything. I did wonder whether, no matter how many thousands of euros had brought prosperity and all those hideous new houses, a country that had seen so much violent death and so much hatred could ever rid itself of ghosts.

The Irish Republic was after all a member of the European Union and everything was supposed to be different but I was never able to forget the day in the Irish pub and the feeling that just under the surface lay something very disturbing.

I enjoyed working for the ICO and I was sad when the time came to an end. We had found a very good young man to take over the sponsorship and, after spending a little while with him, my job was done.

It was at this time that tragedy entered my life again. My son David had been living, on and off, in Australia. He had a very nice wife, Karen, who was a nurse in the intensive care unit of the hospital in Hobart and two daughters, Lauren and Joanna. I had been to visit them on two or three occasions and found Australia a country that I did not like at all. I always thought that it would be rather like South Africa, but it isn't. The fact that South Africa was colonised by the Dutch and the French as well as the British gave it a very different heritage and I found Australia somehow very harsh. There were nice things, of course. I loved seeing my granddaughters; I got on very well with Karen; and they lived near the beach, which meant lovely walks along the water's edge where one could find the most beautiful shells I have ever seen. David had always loved animals and he had a wonderful dog called Spike who used always to accompany him when he went fishing, walking straight into the water as David began to fish and simply swimming around and around until it was time to go home. I loved Spike.

David was immensely creative, a prize-winning sculptor, a painter and latterly he had written poetry which was well received. Good looking and blessed with a very strong physique, he was attractive to women and it was impossible to understand why his life had been such a difficult one. By this time his marriage had very sadly failed and he was living alone in Brisbane. There had been a crisis a couple of years earlier. I had flown to Brisbane to do what I could to help and mercifully things improved and for the time being all seemed well. Then once again I was telephoned to hear that he was desperately ill in hospital having undergone brain surgery and, of course, I went to Brisbane again. Typically, he had allowed a homeless Aborigine to stay in his flat and when the situation became intolerable and he told him to leave, the man had attacked David, forcing his head back by pressing the heel of his hand against David's nostrils, which had caused brain damage.

I arrived to find that David, his head swathed in bandages, was very ill, having undergone two operations to relieve the pressure on his brain. Fortunately his daughter Lauren was able to join me and that was an enormous help, but it was a time of awful anxiety and I was pretty miserable in a rather horrible small hotel in Brisbane. The days passed and miraculously David began to recover, although I did doubt whether he would ever make a complete recovery. Obviously I could not stay indefinitely and eventually, after lengthy conversations with the doctors, I returned home, with David safely settled in a rehabilitation centre. Eventually he was well enough to move to a flat on the Gold Coast and the situation was more or less normal. Polly and Julian went for a holiday to Australia. They saw him and found him fairly well, with his very sharp sense of humour fully in place.

In 2008 he suffered a stroke and was back in hospital. Everyone was so kind to me. I used to telephone every day and although David could not speak, the nurses held the telephone to his ear and I spoke to him while they assured me that he knew it was me and was responding. Both his daughters were with him which was a huge comfort to me but on 18 September David died. Once again, I was surrounded by kindness and support and my parish priest, Father Ray Blake, was incredibly supportive and understanding. I was heartbroken.

MAKING MUSICIANS

Some time after this I happened to be staying with John Owen in his Irish house. We were sitting, chatting idly, and the subject of the Britten–Pears School came up. We both bemoaned the fact that, although every aspect of the Aldeburgh Festival, as well as the lives of Benjamin Britten and Peter Pears, had been written about extensively, no one had produced anything about the School. 'It's so awful,' I said, 'because soon everyone will be dead and there will be nobody left who remembers it all.' 'Well, why don't you do it?' For a moment I was flabbergasted at the idea, and then after a time I thought, 'Well, why don't I?' And that started me on the four-year path that was to lead to the publication of *Making Musicians*.

After deciding to undertake the work, the first person I went to see was Donald Mitchell in his flat in Bloomsbury. Donald was tremendously enthusiastic and said, 'Oh, Moira, how thrilled Ben and Peter would be if they knew what you are doing. The first person you must go and talk to is Colin Matthews.' Colin was equally in favour of the project and said that I had identified a real gap that needed filling. When I said that I knew there would be a lot of travel and that I could not afford it, he replied that he would talk to the Britten–Pears Foundation. In due course he told me that they had agreed to pay my expenses and I started on the mammoth task I had set for myself.

The first research I had to undertake was at the Britten–Pears Library in Aldeburgh and I went there to have my first meeting with Richard Jarman and Chris Grogan. Richard was the general director of the Foundation and Chris was then the librarian. They both seemed very friendly and, given their support, I was able to make a start.

I went to Aldeburgh several times to work in the Library and received nothing but kindness and support. Nick Clark, the assistant librarian, was particularly helpful, as were my old friends Anne Surfling and Pamela Wheeler, the archivists. All seemed to be going well and I prepared for my first visit abroad, which was to Toronto to interview Françoise Sutton, the wonderful Frenchwoman who had started the Canadian Friends of Aldeburgh and raised large amounts of money to send Canadian students to the Britten–Pears School. While in Toronto, I also saw Stephen Ralls and Bruce Ubukata, very old friends of mine, who regularly had been repetiteurs at the School. I was given a warm welcome and wonderful help.

I spent a long time with Françoise who had her own unique memories of the early days of the Festival and of her friendship with Britten and Pears. She generously shared these memories with me, and Stephen and Bruce did the same with all their recollections. A highlight of the visit was being taken to a performance in the new Toronto opera house to which Françoise very kindly invited me and which seemed familiar, as it was based on the architecture of the Glyndebourne opera house.

In addition I was able to see and interview several Canadian musicians who had been students at the School. This was, of course, my second visit to Toronto, the first unforgettable for my embarrassment when the carousel went wrong and I was talking about the Britten–Pears School. I don't think that it was simply as a result of the memory of that embarrassment, but I can't say that I liked Toronto much. Despite the warmth with which I was received, it still seemed to me a lifeless place; everything so neat and tidy, streets well laid out and trees planted, but nothing to show that real people lived there. However, despite the feeling of the lifelessness of Toronto, I thought that my visit was reasonably successful and I returned to England, happy at what had been achieved.

My second journey abroad was to see Hugues Cuénod, the very successful tenor who had taught at the Britten–Pears School regularly; astonishingly he was now a hundred and four years old but still retained his charm and exquisite manners. John Owen and I had twice before been invited to stay with him, so I knew him very well and also knew Alfred, his devoted friend and companion, who now that Hugues was so frail, cared for him with total commitment. I felt almost tearful when, after supper, Alfred gathered him up in his arms and carried him to bed like a beloved child.

At this time they were in Hugues's home in Vevey and I stayed in the rather spooky house, which was old, had been in the family for generations and was in serious need of a bit of modernisation, or anyway a lick of paint. Both Hugues and Alfred were such generous hosts and, although Hugues was indeed very frail, I was able to record my conversations with him and I was pleased with the result. He lived until he was a hundred and eight and on his last birthday he was able to speak to me quite distinctly, when I telephoned to wish him a happy birthday.

Next I went to Moscow as I wanted to talk to Galina Vishnevskaya, Slava's widow, who had been such an important influence at the School and where she regularly directed Russian song courses. I used to see Galina every day when she was in Aldeburgh and had often been lucky enough to enjoy her very Russian hospitality at their house in Aldeburgh, Cherry House – 'My name,' she would say. (*Vishnjya* means 'cherry' in Russian.) It was mainly in Cherry House that she wrote her remarkable autobiography, entitled simply *Galina*. I had read it in translation, but her extraordinary vitality shines out on every page. What a life it was, and I shall never forget her memories of the siege of Leningrad through which she lived, a teenager, alone with her grandmother, who died in the siege, leaving Galina completely alone.

Now a widow in her eighties, obviously ill and showing the effects of the cortisone that kept her alive, she still retained some of her glamour, dressing elegantly and always wearing make-up, ready for anything. I went to Moscow with Nick Winter; it was a great help to be with him because of his fluent Russian. He, too, was keen to see Galina again; he would then go on to St Petersburg to visit friends. And so it was agreed that he and I should travel to Moscow and spend two or three days there, visiting Galina.

She lived in a rather grand house in central Moscow that she had converted into a small opera house, rehearsal studios and administrative offices, retaining for herself a very nice apartment on the top floor. It was a clever arrangement, very typical of Slava and Galina. The house actually belonged to the Moscow authorities, who supported her opera school and gave bursaries to the students. The first night we were there she invited us to the finals of her singing competition and a reception afterwards. The competition was held in the new concert hall, which has beautiful views of the river. Afterwards we went to a hall where the reception was held. There were chairs and tables in the room, which was rather like a village hall on a large scale, and a huge buffet, which all the guests gathered around, apparently eating as much as possible in the shortest possible time. It was a bit of a scrum. Galina sat in a chair at the top of the hall with the chair next to her vacant – 'For Slava.' She had done the same thing in the concert hall and I understood that wherever she went, there was an empty chair kept for Slava.

The following day we went to her house for the interview, with Nick ready to interpret. Galina's English had always been poor. I thought she placed little importance on the language and just couldn't be bothered. We recorded an excellent interview and she told stories of her early friendship with Britten and Pears and of her subsequent work at the School. I think it must be one of her very last interviews. Nick subsequently translated it and recorded his translation on disc.

It was amazing to see her in these circumstances in central Moscow and to think that before he died Rostropovich had been the honoured guest at a reception given by Vladimir Putin. Anyone who has seen the photograph of Slava and Galina after they were informed that they would have to go into exile and seen the agony on their faces will surely never forget it; all those long years that they suffered when they were forbidden entry into the country they loved so much. Slava had signed a letter criticising the regime and this had put him in terrible danger, but Galina told me that the last straw and the reason for their exile was because they offered Solzhenitsyn hospitality in their dacha at a time when he was facing persecution by the authorities.

I know that I saw very little of it, but I hated Moscow. I could not get over the traffic jams and the fact that you faced gridlock if you wanted to go anywhere. I was also dismayed and a bit frightened by the Moscow taxi system. The accepted way to get from A to B is to go and stand in the road, in the thick of the traffic, and wave your arm. A car will stop. It might be a handsome Mercedes or an awful old rattle-trap with doors that don't quite work. A discussion about your destination and the price will ensue and, if everyone is happy, you are expected to climb into the car of a total stranger, unlicensed as a taxi, and sit there happily while you are driven to your destination. Although I was with Nick, I found it all quite terrifying, despite being assured that everyone did it and that everyone understood the system.

On the first day I was there, the pavements were crowded with extremely drunk young men in uniform, carrying bottles, and singing and shouting. I found it intimidating and it was explained to me that each particular branch of the public services is given a day that is their day, when they don't have to work and can get as drunk as they like. I was astonished when I was told that this was Border Guards Day! What with the traffic, the fear of pickpockets, the taxi system and drunken border guards, I thought Moscow was horrible, although I did enjoy a very good Russian dinner in an attractive restaurant with Nick. I was sorry that I could not visit St Petersburg, but it was just not possible.

This was my last visit abroad for the book and from now on all the work for it was at home. As I sat before the blank screen of my computer and wrote for days and days on end, I found the whole project so formidable that I often wondered whether I had bitten off more than I could chew. However, gradually the work was more or less done, and in 2011 I went to Aldeburgh for what turned out to be my last meeting there. I sat in the Red House kitchen with Chris Grogan and Nick Clark and we discussed in considerable detail the plans for publication. They had both read a draft of the whole book. We talked about what would be the best retail price, whether we would go for paperback, who would be the designer. Chris said that he would contact Boydell & Brewer, publishers of the Britten Letters and of Aldeburgh Studies in Music. We went into considerable practical detail.

I had previously asked Jill Burrows, who had had a long association with Aldeburgh and whose work I admired enormously, whether she would edit the book and what she would charge. This was also discussed. Although there had been many hitches along the way, especially when Chris Grogan had been on gardening leave, and endless delays and problems over the budget, which had been nerve-racking and unsettling, I left Aldeburgh on this occasion happy with the result of the meeting. At last, I thought, we are actually getting somewhere and publication was distant but really in sight. I was naive enough to think that we were all, as they say, on the same page.

I had discussed all the earlier difficulties and delays with Jill Burrows and with Philip Reed, who had formerly been the Musicologist at the Britten–Pears Library, and is a highly respected Britten scholar. They had both been supportive and helpful and understood the situation precisely. Kenneth Baird, my boss at Aldeburgh and a very close friend, was also aware of all the ups and downs that had occurred along the way and had given me his total support. I had, however, been heartened by that last meeting and I thought that everything was now moving in the right direction.

I was, therefore, completely unprepared, when, out of the blue, I received a letter from Peter Clifford, the managing director of Boydell & Brewer. I knew who he was but until that moment I had never had any direct contact with him. He wrote that a meeting had taken place between Richard Jarman, Nick Clark and himself to discuss my book. (I was confident that Richard Jarman had yet to read a word of it.) Peter Clifford informed me that it had been decided that the best way forward was to get some unnamed person to write an 'authoritative' book about the School, to include my work. In other words, my work was to be subsumed into someone else's book. I was stunned and I read and reread the letter in disbelief. Would I let him know, Clifford asked, whether I found this an acceptable way to proceed? (I later learned that this letter had been thought so important that it had gone backwards and forwards between the Red House and Boydell & Brewer with the wording being endlessly picked over and redrafted.)

I spoke to Ken, Jill and Philip, who had been so encouraging, and told them that I would reply to say that I found the proposal totally unacceptable. The representatives of the Britten–Pears Foundation seemed to assume that I would be a pushover and just go along with whatever they suggested. I could guess the identity of the person who would be writing the 'authoritative' book about the School, swallowing my work in all likelihood unacknowledged, someone already close to the project and whom I had until this point trusted. This person already 'had form' in absorbing the work of other writers into books with only his own name appearing on the jacket and title page.

When I refused to have anything to do with this idea, which I found offensive and insulting, it truly put the cat among the pigeons. I could not believe that my work, a personal memoir undertaken with the very best intentions and with the support of Donald Mitchell and Colin Matthews, two of the people perhaps closest to Britten's and Pears's own thinking, could cause such a commotion and have such far-reaching impact. To this day, I really do not understand why it became so important to put an end to my plans for a book.

It led to my becoming persona non grata at Aldeburgh and everyone at the Red House was apparently instructed to have no contact with me. I found this particularly hurtful as some of them were such old friends and I thought that they were pretty wet to obey the instruction. Although this diktat applied to the Britten–Pears Foundation, covering the staff at the Red House and the Library, it did not apply to the Aldeburgh Foundation (at the time called Aldeburgh Music) and the Festival. In fact, Jonathan Reekie, then the chief executive of Aldeburgh Music, could not have been kinder or more helpful. He generously gave me an extended interview so that I could bring the story of School right up to date.

The upshot of all this is that Jill, Philip, Ken and I set up a publishing venture of our own, the Bittern Press, and that several very kind, generous friends made donations towards the expense of publication. I had a discussion with Jill and told her that I would very much like to meet Peter Clifford in person. We also hoped that he might be persuaded to help us with the distribution and marketing of *Making Musicians*. Although the infamous letter had been signed by him, I knew that it was unlikely that he had personal knowledge of the book or its contents. So we contacted him and requested a meeting.

I was both surprised and delighted when he agreed and Jill and I set out for Woodbridge and the Boydell & Brewer offices. We were shown into a meeting room where I met Peter Clifford; Jill already knew him. I found him amusing and charming and it was clear that we all got on very well. He said that he wanted to read a draft of the book and Jill, rather anxiously, murmured that it was as yet unedited. 'Jill, I know how to read a draft,' he said. He also told us that Boydell & Brewer never undertook a distribution and publicity deal. 'If we did,' he said, 'we would have a queue right around the building.' We left, after a very good-humoured meeting, having agreed to email him the draft, which he said he would read and discuss with Michael Richards, his marketing director.

I knew that we still had a long way to go, but I felt a degree of elation and believed that all the signs were favourable – at last. I was right and I can hardly describe my delight when Peter Clifford wrote to say that Boydell & Brewer would handle all the publicity and the distribution of the book. *Making Musicians*, the title we had chosen, would appear on all their listings worldwide, and when I saw the distinguished company it would be in, I really did begin to feel great satisfaction and excitement. Everything that I had hoped for was now going to happen.

It was a very exciting time with decisions about design and photographs to be made and long conversations with Jill about the editing. I can never praise her enough and without her help and the help of Kenneth Baird and Philip Reed the book would not have seen the light of day. Finally a publication date was decided – 28 May 2012. We booked the English Speaking Union in Mayfair and began work on the launch. The ESU was an especially happy choice of venue as Britten and Pears had performed there and we had always had ESU-sponsored students at the Britten–Pears School. We invited everyone from the Britten–Pears Foundation and Library who had been involved in the early phases of the project but none of them – except Nick Clark – accepted the invitation. I was still out in the cold.

The launch party was fun. I was very pleased that Graham Johnson, who had generously written the foreword to the book, was there, although I knew that it was the sort of event which he would usually avoid. Iain Burnside introduced me and Philip Reed made a short speech. I was delighted that Colin Matthews was able to be there. Afterwards Ken and I invited to dinner Peter Bowring (formerly the chairman of the Aldeburgh Foundation) and his wife Carole, as well as Derek Sugden and Katherine Douglas (Derek's future wife). Derek, who died at the end of 2015, was one of the foremost acousticians in the world and he had been responsible for much of the success of the Snape Maltings Concert Hall and the Britten–Pears School. When I was researching *Making Musicians*, he was exceptionally kind and helpful and gave me access to photographs and documents.

There was yet to be one further extraordinary event linked to the book, probably the most extraordinary of all. Perhaps bizarre is a better word. In mid-June, the Aldeburgh Bookshop hosted a launch of the book. The Festival was in full swing and the book was also to be on sale in the concert hall bookshop; I was also asked to go to the School where *Making Musicians* was on display. There was a very lively, cheerful crowd in the Aldeburgh Bookshop – happy, I think, to be given a glass of wine. A very satisfactory number of copies was sold. I was pleased that Michael Richards of Boydell & Brewer was there.

I was staying with Rita Thomson, who after Britten's death had remained in the Red House as friend and companion to Peter Pears. She now has her own house in Aldeburgh where I had spent the night. Rita came to the launch, as did Jill Burrows and Philip Reed. As we were leaving, the four of us were standing talking on the pavement outside the bookshop when Philip said, 'Did you see Richard Jarman there?' I was absolutely nonplussed. 'What? Where?' I could not resist going back inside the shop, and there I saw him lurking in the map department, apparently trying to make himself invisible. As far as I was concerned, it was an appropriately ridiculous end to what – in part – had been such an unhappy saga.

With the Aldeburgh book launch over Rita and I had lunch at the Wentworth Hotel, so familiar to me for such a long time, and then I went to Snape, to the School, the most appropriate place of all for an event marking the publication of my book. Bill Lloyd was then the director of the School and he greeted me warmly and kindly and did everything possible to help. Jonathan Reekie was also there and was equally kind and welcoming.

I RETURNED TO BRIGHTON after all the excitement and for a while everything felt rather flat. The book, which had occupied almost all my time for the previous four years, was done and suddenly the days were somewhat empty. When the reviews started to appear, however, that all changed. I had really not expected to be quite so thrilled and I had never experienced anything quite like it. There was all the work I had done, now being discussed by other people; it was a very strange sensation. The magazine *Classical Music* gave it a very good review and, at the end of the year, chose it as one of its books of the year.

In 2013 I became very active again when I decided to move to a different flat a few streets away. Moving is hell at the best of times, but at eighty-eight it is not just hell but almost impossible. 'Oh dear, I do hope that this is not going to kill Moira,' a friend remarked, and at one time I thought it might. But finally settled, and with books on the shelves instead of a mountain of boxes, I looked around for something new to do and with Ken's encouragement, I decided that I would write this story.

The year 2015 saw the occasion of my ninetieth birthday and my grandchildren, Emma and Luke, my daughter Nickie's children, arranged the most wonderful party for me at Scott's in Mayfair. It was not a large party but most of my closest friends were there and nearly all my family; only David's daughters were missing. As I looked around at my friends and my family, including four great grandchildren, I felt that although there have been dreadful experiences to endure, it has also been a wonderful, happy, fascinating and completely unexpected life.

ACKNOWLEDGEMENTS

THERE ARE SO MANY that I must thank for their help with *Change of Key* but my first thanks must go to Kenneth Baird. He was the person who originally suggested that I should write it and throughout the whole process he has been ready with assistance and encouragement, giving the project hours of his own time and making sure that any non-PC expressions I might have used were suitably amended. I am truly grateful to him for all this and for making me laugh throughout it all. I must, of course, thank my editor Jill Burrows for her unfailing help, for the painstaking work and imagination she has put into the design and the editing of this book. I owe a debt of gratitude to my fellow director of Bittern Press, Philip Reed, who has from the beginning been stalwart in his support. There are many others who have helped me and I would like to thank Libby Rice, the LSO Archivist, who went to enormous trouble to find some of the old LSO and Barbican Centre pictures and Rosalyn Wilder, my good friend and former colleague, who let me see and use her collection of old programmes and memorabilia. I must also thank Clare Bowskill, John McLaren and Louise Schweitzer for their help and encouragement; it has been much appreciated. Of course, I also want to thank my own family for their steadfast support, on which I have so much depended. Without the help of all of these *Change of Key* could not have happened and I am truly grateful to all of them.

PHOTOGRAPHIC ACKNOWLEDGEMENTS

THE AUTHOR AND PUBLISHERS gratefully acknowledge the following owners and copyright holders for the use of illustrative material:

Arup: p. 81 (top and lower right); Moira Bennett's personal and family collection: pp. 9, 13–16, 37–40, 82 (top left and right), 106 (lower left and right), 135 (lower left), 160 (top left and right); Graham Johnson: p. 105 (lower left); London Symphony Orchestra Archive: front cover (right), pp. 129, 133, 134, 135 (top, and lower right), 136, 141, 146, 157, 158, 159, 160 (lower); Nigel Luckhurst: pp. 82 (lower left and right), 83, 84, 103, 104, 105 (top left and right, lower right), 106 (top).

While every reasonable effort has been made to identify copyright holders of images reproduced in this book, the author and publishers apologise for any inadvertent omissions and would be pleased to hear from any unacknowledged copyright holders.

INDEX

References to illustrations and captions are shown in *italics*.

188

Moira Bennett gives an insider's perspective on forty years of the Britten–Pears School for Advanced Musical Studies, from ad hoc classes in a grainstore at Snape, through its hectic annual calendar of courses for singers, string players and ensembles alongside fully staged operas, up to its current incarnation as the Britten–Pears Young Artist Programme. Her generously illustrated account is complemented by the memories of former students and members of faculty.

A *Classical Music* magazine Book of the Year, 2012

'Moira Bennett, part of the fixtures and fittings at the school for years, here traces the story with the eye for detail which by all accounts has been a hallmark of her work at Aldeburgh . . . Pears died in 1986, the day after giving a masterclass on the role of the Evangelist in the Bach Passions, building up to the Crucifixion. "But then there was the resurrection," were his final words. This book is, in a way, a form of resurrection – a bringing to vivid life of how Britten's innocent words ["One day we'll have a school here . . ."] bore extraordinary fruit.'

Andrew Green, *Classical Music*

'Bennett's "personal history" – part memoir, part carefully researched record – bubbles with an excitement reflecting the school's evolution from merely an idea in the 1950s, to a new venture in the 1970s and 1980s, to a well-established school with an international reputation by the end of the century . . . Graham Johnson, an accompanist for early masterclasses, describes Bennett as a young "mother of the school" who enchanted Peter Pears and made the school a "happy place" for students and teachers alike.'

Shersten Johnson, *Notes*

Moira Bennett: *Making Musicians*
Bittern Press, 2012
232 pages   133 photographs
ISBN 978 0 9571672 0 9

.